This one's for Bill Schafer

The Matthew Scudder Series:

THE FOUR OF US—Kristin and Mick, Elaine and I—stood on the stoop of their brownstone for the ritual round of hugs. Mick and I settled for a manly handclasp.

"Safe home," he said.

It was a crisp Sunday night late in September, the sky free of clouds, and if we'd been in the country we would have seen stars. But there's always too much ambient light in the city for stargazing, and I suspect that's also true metaphorically. Ambient light, softening the darkness even as it prevents our seeing the stars.

Mick and Kristin's house stands on West 74th Street between Columbus and Amsterdam. It's on the south side of the street, so when we reached the sidewalk we turned to our right and walked the half block to Columbus Avenue, which magically becomes Ninth Avenue when it crosses 60th Street. Under either name, the thoroughfare is southbound, and there's a bus that would drop us right across the street from our apartment.

It was pulling away as we neared the corner.

Elaine said, "What do you want to do? Flag a taxi? Call a Via?"

Via is like Uber, except with shared rides and correspondingly lower prices.

"Whatever you want," I said.

"How's your knee?"

We'd walked up earlier. The Ballous live just under a mile from us, and in good weather we both prefer to cover that distance on foot, but my right knee had ached on the way.

"It's okay now," I reported. "On the way up, it stopped bothering me around the time we crossed 72nd. You feel like walking?"

"I wouldn't mind. But what if your knee decides to act up on the other side of 72nd?"

I said something about crossing that bridge when we came to it, and she said I meant crossing that street, and we walked along chatting like an old married couple, which in fact we had somehow become.

We'd gone a few blocks, with no complaint from

my knee, and had lapsed into a companionable silence. I broke it to say, "When she served raspberry tart for dessert, I got the feeling you were going to talk about your group."

"You picked that up? I almost did, and then I didn't."

"What stopped you?"

"Oh, the conversation took a turn." She fell silent, then broke the silence to say, "No, that's not what it was. I decided the conversation *would* take a turn if I broached the subject, and it was a turn I didn't want it to take."

I nodded, and she said it was a beautiful night and she was glad we'd decided to walk. I agreed with her, and we crossed another street, and my knee begged to differ. You get old and things hurt and then they don't and then they do again.

She said, "I guess I decided to keep it private."

"That's fair enough."

"I could have talked about it without breaking anybody's anonymity but my own. And my misspent youth is nothing Mick and Kristin aren't aware of. But the Tarts, I don't know—"

"You don't have to overthink it," I said. "It's how you felt."

"Your knee's bothering you, isn't it? Let's get a cab."

I shook my head. "It's not that bad. And as close as we are—"

"I married a stubborn man."

"You knew that going in," I said. "And I think 'persistent' is a better word than 'stubborn.' It's less judgmental."

"I was already cutting you some slack with 'stubborn,'" she said. "The first word that came to me was 'pigheaded.' But I decided that really would be too judgmental."

"We're almost home," I said. "See how easy that was?"

"Judgmental or not, you can't say it was inaccurate."

"You're cute when you're judgmental."

"Is that a fact. And we *are* almost home, and the first thing you're gonna do is elevate that leg, and I'll fetch an ice pack. Deal?"

"Deal," I said.

I'VE BEEN SOBER A while. I'd marked thirty-five years in November, as I mentioned at a meeting a day or two after the actual anniversary date.

Whenever anyone expresses surprise over my continuing attendance at AA meetings, I think of the shampoo commercial:

....

"You use Head & Shoulders? But you don't have dandruff."

"Riiight."

I don't go as often as I did early on, but I still manage to turn up more often than not at the 8:30 meeting Fridays at St. Paul the Apostle. When we resumed keeping company—and that, astonishingly, was 28 years ago—Elaine began attending Al-Anon meetings, but the program never really reached her, and she didn't find the companionship there that I did in AA. One night she came home with a definition of an Al-Anon slip: "An unanticipated moment of compassion. And they're pretty rare."

So you could say it wasn't a good fit for her.

Then, a couple of years ago, she heard about the Tarts. It wasn't an acronym for anything, nor was it an official name for the group. It was what some of the members called it, for lack of anything else to call it, and what it was in essence was an anonymous program for women with a prior history of prostitution.

Elaine was in the game when we first met, and that was a lot more than 28 years ago. She was a sweet young call girl and I was a detective with the NYPD, and along with my gold shield I had a wife and two sons in Syosset. I suppose we were in love from the start, although neither of us quite knew it at the time, and it lasted until it ended, and years later when

....

circumstance threw us together again we were ready for it. I had already stopped drinking, and after a year or two she stopped entertaining clients, and now we were this nice elderly couple who still seemed to take delight in one another's company.

I first heard about the Tarts when she came home after her third meeting. "There's this group I started going to," she said. "Girls who used to be in the game."

"A 12-Step program?"

"More or less, but without the twelve steps. One dame tells her story and then we go around the room. I don't know if I really belong there."

"You do," I said, "and you know it."

"Oh?"

"You said, 'And then we go around the room.'"

" 'We' and not 'they.'"

"Uh-huh."

"I think you're right. Actually I think we're both right. I belong there. It's funny, I thought I'd dealt with all of this."

"Tricking."

"Yeah. I've always said that prostitution did a lot more for me than it ever did to me."

"That's just about word for word what Churchill said."

"Churchill? As in Winston Churchill?"

"So I'm told. I wasn't there to hear him say it."

"Winston Churchill was turning tricks?"

"God, there's an image. No, he was talking about booze. 'I know that alcohol has done a good deal more for me than it's ever done to me.'"

"Oh, that's right. I always picture him with a cigar, but he was a heavy drinker, wasn't he? Do you think he was right? About his drinking?"

I said I had no idea. She nodded and got back on track. "The conventional wisdom is that turning tricks lowers your self-esteem, but it elevated mine. I didn't have any self-esteem until I got in the life."

"The game, the life . . ."

"Euphemisms," she said. "Some of the members use them. Others are more in-your-face. 'Until I started selling pussy.' Like that. What are you smiling at?"

" 'In your face.'"

She rolled her eyes. "When I walked into my first meeting, a couple of weeks ago? I was so much older than everybody I thought I was out of place. They were all nicely dressed in skirts and sweaters or tailored jeans. And they didn't look like hookers."

"Whatever that means."

"But then two of them welcomed me and said their names, and another handed me a cup of coffee, so I sat down. Then the meeting started and a woman told her story. She looked like a woman at a bank who'd help you fill out a mortgage application, and she had a story that would take paint off a trailer hitch. Her uncle started messing with her when she was, I don't know, eleven years old? And five years later a pimp turned her out, and she never got in a house or on the phone, she went straight onto the stroll in the East 20s. Blow jobs in cars, mostly, and a couple of times she thought she was gonna get killed, but, you know, she survived. It was a horrible story and nothing like anything in my own experience, and all the same I hung on every word and got a lump in my throat and found myself having to hold back tears."

"You identified."

"I guess. Meetings are Tuesday afternoons at the Croatian church way west on Forty-first Street."

"Easy enough to get to."

"Which is good," she said, "because we're the only group in the city, as far as I know. I went back the next week and again there were all these sweet young things, and I felt like they'd take one look at me and figure I was some demented Church Lady who'd wandered into the wrong room, but then a couple of them remembered me from the week before and said hello and I sat down and the meeting started. Most of them, I'm old enough to be their mother, and there are a couple who could be my grandkids, but for the services of a friendly neighborhood abortionist. But they honestly don't relate to me like I'm a woman in her sixties."

"You realize, of course, that you don't come close to looking your age."

"You're sweet, and I guess that's true, but nobody's going to card me in a gin joint. These women know I'm older but they relate to me like I'm the same age as they are." She cocked her head. "Or maybe that's just something I'd prefer to believe."

"No," I said. "It's probably true. Age disappears in an AA room. We tend to be more aware of length of sobriety than time on the planet."

"This afternoon," she said, "there was a woman who had to be five years older than me. She tried to disguise her age with makeup, and who doesn't, but she overdid it and it had the opposite effect."

"An old-timer?"

"In the life, for sure. But not an old-timer at Tarts. She turned her last trick three or four days ago."

"Jesus."

"If it *is* her last trick, because she's been trying to quit for a while now. She's got this apartment in a full-service building in Murray Hill, and she had one of the porters come up to tell her how much he'd charge her to wash her windows. He quoted her a price, and she said that seemed on the high side, and

he gave her a sly look and told her he figured they
could work something out."

"And I gather they did."

"What is it Mehitabel always says? In *archy and
mehitabel*? 'There's life in the old dame yet.'"

"And she said that?"

"What she said, word for word, was 'So I took
him into the bedroom and fucked his brains out.'"

"I hope he got those windows spotless."

"Oh, that's the best part. Afterward, while he's
lying there with his eyes rolled up into his head, she
tells him to do a good job on the windows and she'll
give him a nice tip. And he did and she did."

"I can see where a person might go to those meetings just for the stories."

"You'd like to be a fly on the wall, huh?"

"Can men come? I could be a retired male hus-
tler."

"That might be a hard role for you to play, honey.
But it's women only. There are other groups for gay
male prostitutes, but you'd probably be less likely to
get off on the stories."

Another time, I expressed some surprise that
staying out of the game could be as hard as making a break in the first place. "I had a client once, a
blonde who got off the bus from Wisconsin and went

straight into the life. She wanted out, and hired me to help convince her pimp to let her go."

"Kim somebody," she said.

"Dakkinen, and I guess I told you about her. The story doesn't have a happy ending."

"She wound up getting killed, but not by her pimp."

"It was a complicated story. But I had the feeling that once I'd assured her she was free to go, that there'd be no hassle from the pimp, she'd be able to leave the life behind."

"And maybe she could have."

"But maybe not? Maybe she could stay chaste until her windows needed washing?"

"Chaste?"

"Well, I don't know the word. What's your group's equivalent of sober?"

"People say different things. Some of the girls say *straight*, but the gay ones don't like that. Some say *righteous*. I'm not crazy about that myself, it's too religious, but it doesn't give me hives. *Clean* means drug-free, and some of us are and some of us aren't, so it doesn't really work. But it may wind up the word of choice, because I've heard it said that you're not really out of the life if you're still taking drugs. Because it's only a question of time before you need to convince a doctor to write a scrip, or you need money for a drug buy."

"Is that how most slips happen? Or do you even call it a slip?"

"A slip, a relapse. Or it's just, 'Well, don't hate me, but I did it again.' But there's less emphasis for us on clean time than there is on sobriety in AA."

"Either way it's a day at a time."

"But numbers matter more in your program, don't they? You have to be sober for ninety days to lead a meeting."

"True."

"Of course we've only been meeting for ten or eleven months. You have the Traditions in AA, don't you? Alongside the Steps?"

"Twelve of each."

"Well, it's hard to develop much in the way of traditions in less than a year." She fell silent for a moment. "I led the meeting last week."

"Oh?"

She nodded. "Told my story."

"All of it? Womb to tomb?"

"From the e-rection to the resurrection," she said. "You were mentioned."

" 'And now, all these years later, I'm married to the guy.' "

"Something like that."

"Seriously," I said, "what did you say?"

"No."

"No?"

She shook her head. "You had to be there."

ELEVATING THE LEG WAS easy enough. There's a recliner in the living room, and I sat down and adjusted the setting appropriately. She brought me the ColdPak that had last seen service a few months ago, when she'd pulled a muscle at a yoga class.

"We should probably have two of these," I said.

"One for each knee? I didn't know they were both acting up. I could wrap ice cubes in a towel."

"No, the other knee is fine. I was thinking one of these for each of us."

"They're not like toothbrushes, honey. It's sanitary to share a ColdPak."

"Well, you can use my toothbrush anytime you want."

"And some people think chivalry is dead."

"The fools they. But what I meant was sooner or later we're both going to be aching at the same time."

She thought it over. "At our age," she said, "we're a two-ColdPak family."

"Sorry," I said. "It was just a passing thought, but once it's spelled out it's kind of depressing, isn't it?"

"Except I like the idea of the two of us growing old together."

"Yes, so do I."

"If I even got to have an old age," she said, "I figured I'd be spending it alone. At some trailer park in Florida, making myself get to the shuffleboard court twice a week, because it doesn't do to let yourself go."

"I've already lived longer than I ever thought I would."

We kicked that around for a few minutes, and then she went to the kitchen and came back with two cups of chamomile tea. I used to drink coffee all day and half the night, and now it's a single cup in the morning. Sometimes two cups, if I'm in a holiday mood.

Depressing or not, depending how you think about it.

IN THE MORNING I was somewhere between asleep and awake when the phone rang. Her side of the bed was empty, so I reached to answer it, but she'd already picked up in the other room. I heard a woman apologizing for such an early call, and Elaine assuring her it was all right, she was glad she'd called. At which point I cradled the phone and decided it was time to get up.

She must have heard the shower, because she had breakfast ready by the time I got to the kitchen. An omelet and a toasted English muffin. I was working on my morning cup of coffee when she said, "Did the phone wake you? I'm sorry, I had my hands full, and it was on its third ring by the time I could pick it up."

"I wouldn't have slept much longer anyway."

"How's your knee this morning?"

"I never thought about it until you just now mentioned it. So I guess it's fine."

She'd made tea for herself in the little Wedgwood teapot. She filled a cup and took a sip, and she said, "That was Ellen Lipscomb."

"On the phone?"

"Uh-huh."

"Is she the one I met? Ellen the Tart?"

A week or so earlier I'd passed the Morning Star, on the northwest corner of Fifty-seventh and Ninth, when I caught a glimpse of Elaine at a table by the far wall. I thought she was by herself, but by the time I'd entered the diner I could see she had company. The woman across the table from her was perhaps half her age, with a pleasing figure and honey-blond hair that fell to her shoulders. I crossed the room and Elaine introduced us, and I said it was nice to meet her.

"Ellen and Elaine," the young woman said. Her

face was pretty, her blue eyes alert. "Just a couple of Ellies, except nobody ever called me that."

"Or me either," Elaine said.

That was about as much conversation as the occasion required, and I said again that it was nice to have met her, and went on to do whatever I'd been on my way to do. When I caught up with Elaine later in the day, I said her friend was attractive and seemed nice.

"Very nice," she said. And after a beat she said, "I know her from meetings."

"You're sure I can't go to those meetings?"

"She's pretty, isn't she? I'm sort of her sponsor."

"Sort of?"

"Well, I haven't heard the term at any of our meetings. But she seems to have picked me out as the more experienced member to seek advice from, and I like her, so I guess you could call that sponsorship."

A fellow named Jim Faber had been my sponsor. We had dinner, just the two of us, every Sunday night for years, always at one or another of the neighborhood's Chinese restaurants. Sometimes but not always we'd cap the evening with a meeting. He was the man I called when I wanted a drink, and after that ceased to be a problem he was the man I turned to when something else in my life was troubling me.

Then one Sunday night twenty years ago he got

killed, shot dead by a man who'd mistaken him for me. I blamed myself for his death, until his voice in my ear finally got through to me and told me all I was guilty of was having to go to the bathroom, and that my guilt was just another form of self-pity. The thought was as annoying as if he'd been standing there and spoken the words aloud, but it got through to me.

The standard recommendation, when your sponsor dies or drinks or moves to New Orleans, is that you find someone appropriate and ask him to take over the role. That's more important and more easily done if you haven't been sober all that long, but when Jim died I had fifteen years, and that made it more difficult to find someone suitable, and less urgent that I do so.

You generally want your sponsor to have more sober time than yourself, and probably to be your age or older. There weren't many men in my home group who emerged as logical candidates, and I told myself I'd get a sponsor when I felt the need, and that never happened. If I had something on my mind that needed discussion, I'd ask somebody or other to join me for a cup of coffee, and we'd have the sort of conversation I might have had with a sponsor. But it was far less formal, and it wasn't the same man each time.

Now, across the breakfast table a few weeks later, I said, "So you're her sponsor."

"Sort of."

"Ellen and Elaine," I said.

"Uh-huh."

"What was it she said? 'Just a couple of Ellies.'"

She rolled her eyes.

"You know," I said, "not that I wish her anything but the best, but if she happens to have a slip, could you let me know?"

"And I'm sure you already know you're a terrible man."

"I do."

"I figured you'd like the looks of her. She's cute, isn't she?"

"Very."

"I could go for her myself," she said, and showed me the tip of her tongue. "But you were already thinking that, weren't you?"

"It may have entered my mind."

"You were imagining yourself in bed with both of us at once," she said. "The old threesome fantasy, except it wouldn't be a fantasy, would it? It would be real, and she'd be right there in our bed between the two of us. And we could do whatever we wanted to her." She ran her tongue around the circle of her lips. Her eyes sparkled, and she put a hand on my thigh.

"We could go back to bed," she said, "and talk about it. Do you think that might be something you'd enjoy?"

AFTERWARDS I GUESS I must have dozed off for a few minutes, and when I opened my eyes Elaine was standing beside the bed with a cup of coffee. "It cooled off," she said, "but I'm happy to see we haven't."

"Jesus."

"Up for breakfast and then back to bed. Well, a nap's a good idea at our age, isn't that what they say?"

"That was some nap."

"It was almost as if we really had her in bed with us," she said, "except it was actually much better, because this way it all turned out the way we wanted it to. They say you should never act out a fantasy because the reality never matches up."

"Is that what they say?"

"It would have to be, don't you think?" She stretched out alongside me, laid a hand on my flank. "Did you have a good time?"

"Do you have to ask?"

"No, and I was right there with you. I think it's marvelous that we're still hot for each other."

"Every once in a while."

"Which is probably about as often as either of us can stand. But we can never ever do this again. You realize that, don't you?"

"Can't do what? Go back to bed? Share an innocent fantasy?"

"We can do both those things," she said. "But we'll have to find other imaginary friends."

"Because she's your sponsee."

"Whatever. What do they call it when a basketball player turns pro after his first year in college?"

"One and done."

"That's Ellen," she said. "As far as we're concerned, she's one and done."

She left the room, and I heard the shower running. Before I knew it she'd hurried back to the bedroom, towel in hand, drying herself frantically. "Oh, shit," she said. "How'd it get to be a quarter to eleven?"

"What's wrong?"

"She'll be here in fifteen minutes."

"Who will?"

"Who do you think? Ellen."

"As in one and done? She's coming here?"

"That's why she called." She scurried around the room, picking up garments, putting them on. It can take her a couple of hours to get dressed, or it can take her five minutes.

"If she'd come over a little while ago—"

"Don't even think it. In fact don't think anything, get under the shower and then put some clothes on."

"You know," I said, "it's probably just as well if I don't see her today. Can't you just take her across the street for coffee?"

"No."

"Or if she's tired of the Morning Star, the Flame's just one block away." She was shaking her head. "Why not?"

"Because she needs to see you."

"Me?"

"That why she called, that's why I told her to come over around eleven. She's got a problem but you'll have to wait for her to tell you about it. I know you already took a shower but—"

"I need another."

I showered, and had the shave I hadn't bothered with earlier. I got dressed, more for comfort than for style, in a pair of jeans and a plaid flannel shirt from L.L. Bean, the one Elaine says makes me look like a lesbian. Maybe if I wore it they'd let me join the Tarts.

I changed it for a blue button-down from Lands' End, tucked it in, and wondered why I was stalling for time. Then I took myself to the living room, where a fresh pot of tea sat on a tray in the coffee table. Elaine and her sponsee sat a few feet apart on the couch, each with a cup of tea. There was a third cup waiting for me, and I filled it and walked over to the recliner. When it wasn't reclining it was just a chair, and I sat in it and took a sip of tea.

Elaine said, "Matt, you remember Ellen."

All too well, I thought.

"From the Morning Star," I said.

"That's right," she said.

"We have a problem," Elaine said, "that's more in your area of expertise than mine."

Which had to mean young Ellen had come to realize she was an alcoholic, so could I take her to a meeting? And maybe introduce her to some women whose company she might find agreeable? Which would retroactively make her unwitting role in our fantasy equally inappropriate for both of us.

"You were a policeman," Ellen said. "And then a private detective? Did I get that right?"

And a remarkably skilled one at that, I thought, quick to mistake a police problem for alcoholism.

She started to say something, then looked over at Elaine, as if hoping for assistance. The only help she got was a nod, but evidently that was enough.

"There's this man," she said.

"Not a pimp," Elaine said for clarification.

"No, nothing like that. A client."

I waited.

"He doesn't want to take no for an answer," she said. "I told him I wasn't seeing guys anymore, and he said he was glad to hear it. I thought he'd be saying what a lot of my johns, my clients—"

"Matt knows the terminology," Elaine said.

"What a lot of them said, when I told them I was out of the life, was they thought that was good. Oh, they might miss me, but I was too nice a person to earn my living by fucking strangers. Um, they didn't put it that way, but—"

"But that was what it amounted to."

"Uh-huh. Anyway, I was ready for that conversation, or some version of it, but what he went on to say was that it had always bothered him a little that I was seeing other men, and how glad he was that I would be seeing him exclusively."

"What gave him that idea?"

"Nothing. I mean, he pretended that was his understanding of what I'd told him. But what he was doing, he was saying that I could clean up my act all I wanted, just so he could keep coming over and going to bed with me."

"Did you straighten him out?"

"He didn't give me the chance. 'Look, just having

this conversation is getting me all hot and bothered, Ell. I'll be there in fifteen minutes, and anything you've got to tell me can wait until then.'"

" 'Ell,'" Elaine said.

"One of the first dates we had, he asked what people called me. I said Ellen, everybody calls me Ellen. 'Well, I'm gonna call you Ell.' And that's what he's called me ever since."

I said, "Staking a claim."

"I guess. Calling me something nobody else called me, so he wasn't just another John. But it's not like what he wanted was the Girlfriend Experience."

Elaine: "That's really a thing, huh?"

"Uh-huh, but mostly with men under thirty." I must have looked lost, because she explained it for me. "The guy's a client, and in fact the fee's payable in advance, so it won't spoil the end of the evening. And you go out and have dinner, and maybe hit a couple of clubs, and you're both putting on an act, like you're boyfriend and girlfriend."

"Putting on an act," I said. "For whose benefit?"

"His, mostly. Or if you go places where they know him, he gets to be seen with this hot-looking chick who's obviously crazy about him. He'll introduce you, because why not, you're boyfriend and girlfriend. But being seen isn't necessarily a part of it. He may just want you to be his girlfriend and relate to him that way for the evening."

"And at the end of the evening?"

"You take him home and fuck him. But it's, you know, romantic, with a lot of kissing along the way, and maybe part of the act is he's got to work a little to seduce you."

"But somehow he always manages," Elaine said.

"Well, duh, of course. I think part of the appeal is he gets to pretend you're on a date but he doesn't have to worry about how the evening's gonna end. He won't wind up going home and jerking off to PornHub. He's a cinch to get laid."

"The Girlfriend Experience," I said.

"A new wrinkle in the world's oldest profession," Elaine said. "I never even heard the phrase until somebody said it at a meeting. I got the impression that it's mostly something everybody knows about and nobody's actually done."

"It's not that rare," Ellen said. "I mean, I've done it."

"Oh?"

"A young guy. I think it's mostly young guys. Unattached, and probably not all that self-confident with women. This one lived in Williamsburg but he was more of a geek than a hipster. Computers, tech stuff. I guess he did okay at it because I told him I'd really love to be his girlfriend but for all those hours I'd need to have a thousand dollars."

"And he paid it?"

"Without a whimper. And it was fine, really, and he took me to the Gramercy Tavern for a great dinner and bought a nice bottle of wine, and it didn't bother him when neither of us had a second glass of it. Then we walked a few blocks and talked, and then we got a cab to my place and made out all the way home."

"Made out," Elaine said.

"Like kids. And he paid the cab and walked me up the stoop, and I think we held hands on the way, and while I'm getting the key in the door he's like, 'You know, Ellen, I've had a wonderful time. And if you want the evening to end right here, I want you to know I'm all right with that.'"

"And you said, 'The part of the evening you paid for is over. And now what I want is for you to come upstairs and have sex with me.'"

"I don't think I said 'paid'. More like 'the part of the evening we arranged.' But the rest is just about word for word."

I asked Elaine how she'd known that.

"Because that's what I would have done," she said. "Might as well give the guy the full Girlfriend Experience."

"If I said I had a great time but I'd prefer it if he left, he'd have gone. I'm pretty sure of it. He'd have been disappointed, but I don't think he'd have kicked up a fuss. But, you know, he was a nice guy and it was a nice evening, so why ruin it for him? And do you want to know something?"

"By this time you really wanted to fuck him."

"Yes! Not for the sex, but because it was the right way for the evening to end. And because it was nice being his girlfriend."

All of this was interesting, even fascinating, but we'd wandered a long way from the real subject. I said, "But this fellow on the phone, he never wanted you to be his girlfriend."

"No, he wanted a working girl. 'Do this, do that.' What he wanted us to do was mostly vanilla, but I was getting paid and he wanted me to earn my money."

"And what did he want now?"

"To come over. To have sex with me."

Elaine: "I don't suppose you told him to shit in his hat."

Ellen grinned. "I don't think I've ever told anybody that," she said, "although I have to admit I like the way it sounds." She turned to me. "I didn't tell him anything. He didn't give me the chance. 'I'll be there in fifteen minutes.' *Click!* End of conversation."

"And he was there fifteen minutes later?"

"Downstairs with his finger on the buzzer. One long and two short, so I would know it was him. Believe me, I already knew it was him."

"And?"

"I buzzed him in. And when he knocked on my door I opened it, and I made him the cup of coffee he asked for, and when he said, 'C'mon, sweetie. I want to fuck you—'"

"You let him," Elaine said.

"I didn't know what else to do. At every stage, I never knew what else to do. On the phone, and when he buzzed, and when he knocked on my door, and when he asked for the coffee. Every step along the way I heard *No* in my mind, and I kept on saying *Yes*."

"All the way into the bedroom."

"And onto the bed." She looked at me, as if it was important that I understand. "It was easier," she said, "to go along than to say no to him. And he was so confident, so sure we were going to do things his way. And, you know, he's a big man, and I don't know if he's strong but he looks strong. If he really wanted for us to have sex, what could I do about it?"

"Fucking him," Elaine said, "was playing it safe."

"Was it? That's what I thought at the time, but maybe I was wrong. Maybe a firm *No* would have sent him home."

"And maybe it would have got you raped, with a beating thrown in."

I said, "What happened when he was done? Did he pay you?"

"He was a regular two hundred dollar trick. He got his wallet from his pants and very deliberately put three hundred-dollar bills on the bedside table. And waited for me to be surprised. I guess my reaction wasn't good enough, because he said, 'A little extra, Ell.'"

" 'Ell,' " Elaine said.

" 'A little extra, because you're not seeing other men anymore.' I said that was very nice of him."

"You were still scared."

A nod. "I didn't know what he would do. From the phone call on, I didn't know what he might do." She took a breath. "What he did was finish dressing. I pulled on my jeans and a blouse, and he said, all matter-of-fact, that next time he was going to do me in, uh, you know."

Elaine: "Macy's window?"

That surprised Ellen, and she laughed a little more than the line deserved. "Oh, God, that's funny! In my, you know."

"In your ass."

"I don't know why I couldn't say that just now. Yes, he was going to fuck me in the ass. I said what I always say, that I couldn't possibly do that with him because his dick was way too big. That usually works, they're too happy hearing that to care that they don't get to—God dammit, why can't I fucking say it?"

We waited.

"That they don't get to fuck me in the ass," she said.

"How did he react?"

"He just grinned and said it wouldn't be a problem. After the first couple of times I'd be nicely broken in. So I said it was something I really didn't care for. That I just didn't like it."

"What did he say?"

"That I didn't have to like it. That all I had to do was take it."

"What a prince," Elaine said. "And then he left?"

"I walked him to the door. Then he turned around and took me by the shoulders and kissed me on the mouth. I don't do that."

"No, of course not."

"Except for the Girlfriend Experience, but that was different. I can't explain how, but—"

"But it was," I said. "He kissed you and then what?"

"I was shocked. I just stood there. And he said he could do that now, because now he didn't have to worry where my mouth had been."

She lost it then, and started to weep. I got out of there and gave Elaine a chance to comfort her in private.

BY THE TIME I came back Ellen had regained her composure, and Elaine was filling all the cups with tea. I took a sip of mine and said, "Once he was out of there, I hope you moved."

"I was out of my apartment within the hour. I threw some things in a gym bag and caught a cab to a hotel. The hotel was too expensive but I had his three hundred dollars, didn't I?"

"That couldn't last long at a New York hotel."

"Not even two days. More like a day, what with room service, which I ordered when I got hungry. A Caesar salad and some coffee, and I think they charged me twenty-five dollars for it."

"But you didn't want to leave the hotel."

"I didn't even want to leave the room," she said. "When room service knocked on the door, I was afraid to open it."

"You're not still at the hotel."

She shook her head. "I have some money saved up," she said, "because I didn't want to get out of the game and then go hungry. I took whatever cash I had in the apartment, and there's more money in my account at Chase. So I could have stayed at the hotel, for a while anyway, but I hate to throw money away." Her eyes locked with mine. "I have to work too hard for it," she said.

"What did you do?"

"After one night in the hotel I called the same real estate agent who'd found me my place on East 27th. That was four years ago, close to five, but he still remembered me. Or at least he pretended to."

"You'd be hard to forget," Elaine said.

"You're sweet, but I look in the mirror and what I see is a blank canvas. You know, kind of pretty but basically generic."

"That's all you see?"

"Pretty much. Who knows, maybe all this shit will put some character in my face."

"So it shouldn't be a total loss," Elaine said.

I said, "When did you hear from him again?"

"He had something to show me that afternoon, a six-month condo sublet on West End Avenue. Fully furnished, down to the linens and towels and the books on the bookshelves, and all I had to do was sign the lease. I moved in right away."

Elaine: "I think Matt was asking when you next heard from Mr. Perfect."

I nodded. "Because if you didn't," I explained, "there wouldn't be a problem."

"Oh, right. I was still there in my head with the real estate guy. I don't know, two days? Three days? The phone rang and there he was."

"The phone in the new apartment?"

"The owners had disconnected it when they went overseas. He's on sabbatical, he's a tenured professor at Columbia. Comparative linguistics, and I don't even know what that is."

"You'll find out," Elaine told her. "All you have to do is read all the books on the shelves."

I said, "He called your cell."

"That's right. That's the only phone I've had in a couple of years, ever since I realized it didn't make any sense to go on paying for a landline."

"So your phone rang and you answered it."

She shook her head. "I recognized his number when it showed up on the screen. I let it go to voice mail."

"He leave a message?"

"Not that time. An hour later he did. 'Can't get you out of my head, Ell.'"

"But you didn't take that call either."

"No, I've never taken a single one of his calls. In fact I never answer the phone, because how do I know it isn't him using a different phone with a number I don't recognize? I check my voice mail, and when it's somebody I want to talk to I call them back, and if they don't leave a message it's probably a rob-ocall anyway. My big chance to save on a time-share in Puerto Vallarta."

I asked if his messages had changed.

"At first they got graphic. This was what we would do when we got together, di dah di dah di dah. And then there was a threat, but only the one time."

"What kind of threat?"

" 'You're a very pretty girl but that could change.' "

"But that was the only threat."

She nodded. "But from the look on your face that's bad news. I thought it was good, that the threats stopped. It's not?"

"Maybe it is," I allowed. "But maybe it means he doesn't want to leave evidence."

"Evidence," she said.

"On your phone. Did you keep the messages?"

"God, I'm so stupid! I deleted every one as soon as I'd listened to it. I wanted to delete them without listening, to keep myself from having to listen to him, but I decided I had to know if he was, you know—"

"Getting close," Elaine said. She leaned forward. "Honey," she said, "you don't want to let this go any further than it already has. I think the first thing you have to do is get an order of protection against him."

"I can't."

"Sure you can. It's a simple procedure, you don't even need a lawyer, though you can have one with you if you want. All you do is—look, if you're afraid it'll piss him off—"

"She doesn't know his name," I said. They both looked at me, and I said, "That's it, isn't it?"

"I know him as Paul," Ellen said. "He never gave me a last name, and as far as that goes I don't think his first name is really Paul. He was telling me some story, and I referred to him in the third person. 'And what did Paul think about that?' Something along those lines. And it took him a beat to get it, as if the name Paul didn't register."

I asked if she had any idea what his name might be. She said she didn't. Elaine said it was probably Rumpelstiltskin, and was a name an absolute requirement for an order of protection? I said I thought it must be, that I'd never heard of one aimed at John Doe, or To Whom It May Concern.

Elaine said, "You know, do those things do any good anyway? On *Dateline*, it seems as though the next thing that happens after somebody gets an order of protection is she disappears, and the whole town is walking through the woods, looking for her and calling her name. Oh, God, honey, nothing like that's gonna happen to you. I watch too much TV, I was just running off at the mouth."

Ellen had gone white, and looked as though she might lose it. But she was hanging in there.

I said, "The fact of the matter is that an order of protection allows you to press charges against anybody who violates it. It's not of much use if there's any actual danger."

She asked if I thought there was.

"I think you have to act as though there is. At this point it's just a matter of phone calls, so it's not as though he's actually stalking you, but—"

"Yes it is."

"Oh?"

"The last call, just this morning. That's why I panicked and called here. 'You moved away, Ell. Why'd you go and do that?' And then he said something about how could I move out and leave the dishes on the table? And didn't I want to come back for my alligator purse?"

"And did you leave dishes on the table?"

"That's what a hurry I was in. And the alligator bag was on a shelf in the bedroom closet. He had to be in the apartment, he had to go into the bedroom and open the closet door, in order to say that."

I asked if the message was still on her phone.

"God, I'm so fucking stupid . . ."

Elaine told her she wasn't stupid, she was scared, and she had every reason to be scared. When I'd left the room earlier, I'd stuck a notebook in my back pocket. I took it out now and uncapped a ballpoint.

I said, "Let's figure out what you know about him."

"But I don't know anything! All I know is his first name and it's probably not even his."

I told her she knew more than she realized.

FOR ONE THING, SHE knew his phone number. Knew it by heart, in fact, but to make sure she checked her phone contacts and confirmed it. The area code was 917, which meant that it was a local mobile phone.

"I never thought of that," she said. "Can you track a person if you know his phone number?"

You can if you're a cop, or know a cop who owes you a favor. I'd been the first and had known plenty who stayed on the job after I left, but every day my contacts faded further into the past. Everybody I ever worked with had retired long ago, and if their names came up at all it was apt to be on the obituary page. When I was working as a private investigator, I'd cultivated younger cops I met in the course of my work, and made a point of staying in touch with them. But most of them had retired by now, and I'd lost touch with the others.

All I said was the technology existed, but that it only worked on a registered phone.

"It might be a burner," Elaine explained, and defined that as a phone purchased anonymously, with prepaid minutes. You could use it for one specific purpose, and discard it when you were done, and there was no record to connect it to its actual user.

"I'll see what I can find out," I said. "Let's see what else you know about him. How old is he?"

"I'd say early forties. But I'm not that good at telling a person's age."

"But no less than thirty-five and no more than fifty?"

"I'd say so, yes."

"Height?"

"Six-one, six-two."

"Weight?"

"I don't know what men weigh. I mean, I don't know how to guess."

"Was he fat? Thin? What kind of body did he have."

She brightened; here was something she could answer. "He was carrying a few extra pounds," she said, "but he was muscular, you could tell he worked out."

"Tattoos?"

"No."

"Scars?"

"None that I noticed."

"Facial hair?"

"No."

"Full head of hair? Or was he balding?"

"He was getting the beginning of a bald spot." She touched the crown of her own head. "Just the beginning. I don't know if he was aware of it."

"Hair color?"

"Brown. A dark brown."

"Any gray in it?"

"Not that I saw. Of course I wouldn't know if Just For Men had something to do with that."

"Guys really use that?"

"Oh, God," Elaine said. "No, nobody uses the stuff. That's why every drugstore in America makes a point of carrying it."

"I guess what I mean is that nobody I know, no *man* I know, dyes his hair."

Elaine said I was wrong, and named the cashier at the Flame. I asked which one, and she said he worked weekday afternoons, wore horn-rimmed glasses. I said, "Marvin? He dyes his hair? How can you tell?"

"Sometimes the roots give him away. Anyway, it's too black."

"If you say so." To Ellen I said, "Dark brown hair. How long? How does he comb it?"

And so on. I asked, she answered, and I wrote in my notebook.

"Where does he live?"

"He never said."

"Nothing about his neighborhood? How he walked to the Museum of Modern Art? What train he took to Yankee Stadium?"

"No."

"How'd he get to your place?"

"By cab, I think."

"And he went home the same way when he left?"

"As far as I know."

I picked up a little hesitation. "What?"

"One time he looked at his watch, then took out his phone and did something. I think he was calling an Uber. Or, I don't know, Lyft. Whatever it was, he did it all on his phone app."

We kicked that around but it didn't go anywhere. I asked if he was a native New Yorker.

"He never said."

"But he said other things, and he said them in his voice. Did he have an accent?"

"Not like a foreign accent, no."

"Southern? Midwest? Bronx? Brooklyn?"

"He just sounded American," she said, and thought about it. "He wasn't from New York."

"You sound certain, Ellen, and a minute ago you didn't know what kind of accent he had."

"I still don't. Something he said. 'For all the years I've lived in this town.' He said it like he'd moved here from someplace else."

Like that narrowed it down, I thought. Half the city's population had moved here from someplace else.

"Is he married?"

She didn't think so. "He didn't wear a ring, and he didn't have that mark on his finger that you get when you take your ring off. I never heard him say anything that suggested he had someone waiting at home for him. He never mentioned children."

I was going to ask what he did for a living, but she beat me to it. "I don't think he has a job," she said. "I think he's self-employed."

"Doing what?"

"Running his own business. I'm just guessing, but he's used to giving orders."

"He ever talk about business?"

"No."

"The pressures of work, anything to give you an idea what his work was?"

"Not that I can think of."

"How about recreation? He play golf?"

"He never mentioned it."

"Any other sports?"

"Not as a participant. One day he said he had tickets for the Knicks that night, that somebody had given him courtside seats. But there was nothing that suggested he went regularly, or that he even cared much about the team. Or the game."

"Tickets. He say who he was going with?"

"No."

"I don't suppose he invited you."

"Why would he do that?"

Elaine: "Maybe he wanted the Girlfriend Experience."

"No, that wasn't what he wanted. I'd already given him what he wanted." She frowned. "*Sold* him what he wanted. He liked paying. He liked taking the bills out of his wallet and handing them to me."

"Always the same amount."

"Two hundred dollars. Always a pair of hundred-dollar bills."

"Until the other day."

She nodded. "When he gave me three of them."

ON AND ON. THE details piled up, and a picture failed to emerge. I knew things about Paul, but I could be in the same subway car with him and not know it.

The same elevator, even.

More questions, more responses, and when I sensed we were spinning our wheels I capped my pen and closed my notebook. Ellen said she'd better get home.

"As in West End Avenue," Elaine said.

"Don't worry. I'm not going anywhere near 27th Street."

"I'll go downstairs with you. I could use some fresh air, and that'll give Matthew a moment to read his notes and exercise his police mentality."

I wasn't sure what a police mentality was, or how to go about exercising mine if I had one, but Elaine was back in no time at all. "I tucked her into a cab," she reported, "and away she went. I didn't see anybody lurking, but would I have noticed?"

"Probably not."

"I said I'd see her tomorrow at the meeting. And I told her to call anytime, any hour, day or night."

"Good."

"This guy Paul. It's got to be a power trip, right? 'You can quit the life but you can't quit me.'"

"Something like that."

"But if he can't find her, and she never answers her phone, sooner or later he'll get tired of it and find someone else who knows the value of two hundred dollars."

I didn't say anything.

"Well? Won't he?"

"Maybe."

"But you don't think so."

"I hope so," I said, "but I don't think so, no."

"Neither do I, but I couldn't tell you why. He's never been violent with her."

"No."

"Or physically abusive. But his last words to her, or almost, were how next time they're going to do anal."

"And he doesn't care if she doesn't like it."

"In fact," she said, "that increases the appeal for him. I don't like where this is going."

"No."

"If she sees him again, and if she lets him do what he wants to do—"

"She's not going to see him again."

"We can't know that, honey. I don't know how close the parallels are to sobriety, but—"

"But she could have a relapse."

"He could find her. He's already found a way to

get into her old apartment, and how do you figure he managed that?"

"Swiped a spare key when she wasn't looking. Slipped one of his famous hundred-dollar bills to her super. Or found a way into the building—"

"Ringing doorbells until somebody buzzed him in."

"That's one way. That would get him to her door, and he might have the talent to get through it. She was in a hurry. Maybe she just closed the door, let the snaplock engage."

"And didn't bother to use her key and turn the deadbolt."

"A lot of snaplocks, especially on doors in old buildings, aren't all that much of a challenge. You could pick one with a butter knife."

" 'You didn't take your alligator bag,' That is so creepy."

"And if he's clever enough to pull that off—"

"Then he's clever enough to track her down?" She made a face. "Maybe he is. Say he could catch up to her, and she could tell herself it was simpler and easier to fuck him one more time than to find some way to get rid of him. And of course he'd insist on anal, because she let him know she doesn't like it. And they'd do it, and the next thing on his agenda is to find something else that she doesn't like. And do it."

"Or she could refuse, and he could rape her."

"Trust you to look on the bright side," she said. "Darling, what are you going to do?"

"The only thing to do," I said, "is find him and stop him. I just wish I knew how to do that."

"IN A MOVIE," she said, "this is when one person suggests going to the police, and the other person explains why that's a bad idea."

"It depends on the movie. Sometimes this is when they do in fact go to the police, and guess what?"

"It turns out to be a bad idea."

"It has to," I said, "or there's no movie. But I'd hand this off to the cops in a hot second if I thought it would do any good."

"But you don't."

"I know how a cop would see it. She's a working girl, and she had some kind of disagreement with one of her customers, and she's set on making trouble for him by going to the cops. So he'd take her statement and make a lot of notes and send her home, and he'd forget her ten minutes after she was out the door."

She thought about it. "It might be different," she said, "if the cop was a woman."

"It might," I agreed, "but it might not. Say

'working girl' to a male cop and the first thought that comes to mind is 'I can probably fuck her.' What would a female police officer think?"

"Well, if she's dykey—"

"No, let's say she's not. She's married herself or she's single and between relationships, and either way she puts in long hours on the job, long dangerous hours, and here's this snooty bitch wearing nicer clothes than she owns and working a couple of hours a day and fucking men just like her husband or her ex or, I don't know—"

"Her father."

"Whatever. So a woman cop might be more sympathetic, but it's not a given."

She thought about it. Did I want a cup of tea? I didn't, and she decided that neither did she. We hadn't had lunch. Was I hungry? I said I wasn't but she should go ahead, and she said she wasn't all that hungry herself and it wouldn't hurt her to miss a meal.

She said, "So what can we do if we can't go to the cops? Say she's a complete stranger and she comes up to your table at Armstrong's and sits down and tells you her story. Then what?"

"Armstrong's," I said. "Jimmy died, what is it, fifteen years ago?"

"Is it that long?"

I did the math in my head. "Longer. Sixteen years.

But I get the point. If I was still in business and she was a stranger, what would I do?" I answered my own question. "Probably walk her over to Midtown North," I said, "and sit her down with Joe Durkin or somebody like him, and make sure they took her seriously."

"You could have done that."

"Back then, sure. Now if I want to sit her down next to Joe Durkin, I'd have to fly her to Florida. And that's assuming he's still alive."

Mortality, never more than half a thought away.

I said, "Let's stop trying to figure out what I would have done twenty years ago. What would I do now?"

"Well?"

"The first order of business," I said, "is getting a name and an address for the son of a bitch."

"Paul."

"Paul whose name probably isn't Paul. I'd want to know his name and where he lives. I wish I had a photo of him, something more than dark brown hair and the beginnings of a bald spot."

"And if you did?"

"I'd show it around her neighborhood."

"Which one? Curry Hill or West End Avenue?"

Curry Hill's what they call those blocks in the East Twenties replete with inexpensive Indian restaurants. The name's a play on Murray Hill, which begins a few blocks to the north.

"I was thinking 27th Street," I said, "but I'd show it around her new neighborhood too, while I was at it. On the off-chance that he'd managed to track her that far."

"So you'd go knock on doors."

"Not these days," I admitted. "These days I get tired thinking about it. I'd get somebody to do it."

"Somebody like TJ?"

"If only," I said.

TJ WAS A BLACK street kid I'd met on Times Square, when a particularly nasty case had me checking out the peep shows and adult bookstores. He'd noticed me and figured I was looking for something, and figured too that he might turn a buck helping me find it. In not much time he became a part of my life—and eventually Elaine's—and remained so for years.

He was somewhere between sidekick and assistant. I'd been living in a hotel at the time, and when I moved in with Elaine across the street at the Parc Vendome, I kept that room as an office. But I spent less and less time in that hotel room, and the day came when I gave it to TJ.

I don't know where he lived before then. He kept a lot to himself.

I did some more mental math, and I said, "Do you know how old he is now?"

"No. But you're gonna tell me, and it won't make me happy."

"He was probably fourteen when I met him. Wiser than his years, certainly, but chronologically something like fourteen or fifteen. He's got to be forty now."

"No. That's impossible."

"Thirty-nine, forty, forty-one. Somewhere in there."

"Oh, I know you're right. I just can't get my mind around it. In my head he'll be a boy forever. Remember his rhyming slang?"

" 'When we gone eat? 'Cause I be starvin', Marvin.' "

" 'So let's do it, Prewitt.' "

" But that was early on," I said. "It didn't take him all that long to let go of that."

"You're saying he outgrew it, Prewitt?"

I gave her a look. "He grew up," I said. "Went through changes, but never quit being TJ. It was pretty wonderful to watch, really."

Across the street at his computer, day-trading stocks. Uptown at Columbia, slipping into classrooms and getting more out of the lectures than the kids whose parents were paying a few hundred dollars a credit. Most of the professors didn't notice he was there. Most of the ones who did were happy to let him stick around.

After he'd been doing this for a few years, a history professor called him over after class. "What you really ought to do," he told him, "is audit Carter Hartwell's class on the Reconstruction era. He gets into stuff we just glide over."

TJ didn't recognize the name.

"He's at NYU. I'm sure he wouldn't object to a bright young man sitting in the back of the room and hanging on to his every word. You know what? I'll make a phone call."

So he took courses, not for credit, at both universities, and by his mid-twenties he'd been in and out of more classrooms than the maintenance staff. More than one professor had said it was a shame he hadn't been a matriculated student all along, that he'd have a doctorate by now. And instead, what did he have? A high school diploma?

Not even that. He'd skipped high school altogether. After eighth grade, he'd bided his time until, just out of curiosity, he turned up at Columbia.

"IF YOU HAD A photograph of Paul," she said, "you could give it to TJ."

"If he was still a teenager."

" 'If we had some eggs,' " she said, " 'we could have ham and eggs, if we had some ham.' You're sure you don't want lunch?"

"Positive."

"Coffee? Anything?"

"No."

"Is there any way to get a photo of the son of a bitch?"

"How?"

"I don't know. Find a place to lurk and when he turns up whip out your phone and take his picture."

"I'd have to take everybody's picture," I pointed out, "because I wouldn't be able to recognize him."

"Because for that we'd need a photo."

"Right."

"And it's too late to give it to TJ, anyway, because somehow or other that little boy got to be forty years old. What happens to the years, anyway? Where do they go?"

"Wherever it is," I said, "they don't come back. How did I get so old?"

"Same way I did."

"No, you're still a sweet young thing. I'm an old man."

"Oh, I don't know," she said. "A few hours ago you seemed pretty young. Vigorous, even."

"Vigorous."

"Uh-huh. I remember something you said about old age."

"That it's a pain in the ass?"

"No, it was something you heard at a meeting, and you liked it enough to bring it home to me. How it's a privilege."

I remembered. "It was downtown," I said. "I was at Perry Street. What was I doing there?"

"Oh, gee, I don't know. Staying sober?"

"Raymond Gruliow, Esquire. Hard-way Ray, except at Perry Street he's known as Ray G."

"Because anonymity is everything."

"He was speaking and he invited me to come down and hear his qualification. Was it his anniversary? It may have been."

"And he said the line?"

"No, but he liked it well enough so that we talked about it afterward over coffee. It was during the discussion, and a woman spoke up. 'Old age is not a burden. It is a privilege denied to many.' What was her name?"

"Does it matter?"

"I can picture her," I said, "and if I were an artist

I could draw her face. She grew up in northern New England, Maine or Vermont. She was a librarian."

"Marian the Librarian?"

"No, but that came to mind because her name was Mary. 'Old age is a privilege denied to many.'"

"It's probably good for us to remember that," she said. "Every once in a while." She frowned. "Something you said."

"Something I said?"

"God, I hate when that happens. Something you said triggered a thought, and then the conversation went on, and the thought got lost. What were we saying?"

"Mary the Librarian," I said. "Old age. A privilege, not a burden."

"Before that."

"How far back? You said I was vigorous for an old man on his last legs."

"Well, you are. But that's not it. Perry Street, anonymity, Ray's anniversary. How many years has he got now?"

"Four."

"That's all? And what's so funny?"

"The traditional response is 'Isn't that wonderful,' not 'That's all.'"

"I just thought he'd been going to meetings a lot longer than that. Oh, I guess he's had relapses."

"It took him a little while to get his footing," I said, "and then he picked up a drink again. The circumstances were in his qualification. He met this attractive European woman at a conference, and the conversation just sparkled, and she said, 'Why don't we have a glass of wine?' And he didn't want the wine, but he didn't want to kill the mood, either. And by the end of the evening he was in a fake Irish pub on Columbus Avenue, knocking back the Bushmill's while all the other drunks hung on his every word."

"And the attractive European woman?"

"Left the meeting with her girlfriend."

"These things happen."

"But he's sober now," I said, "and as of that meeting he had four years, but it must be closer to five by now."

"Five years," she said "Isn't that wonderful?"

HALF AN HOUR LATER she came over to where I was sitting. She had a dish towel in one hand and a coffee cup in the other, and she said, "Ray G."

"As in Gruliow. What about him?"

"Not him," she said. "The other Ray G."

"Oh, for Christ's sake."

"I had the thought and I couldn't find my way

back to it. And then a minute ago it was just there, and I wanted to tell you before it went away again. But I'm pretty sure it won't at this point, and now I've told you, so—"

"Are they still living in Williamsburg?"

"As far as I know. And I would think he'd still have the same number. I can look it up."

But it was in my phone's list of contacts. I made the call.

TUESDAY MORNING I AWOKE from a dream and when I got back from the bathroom I decided I wanted to get back into it. I couldn't find my way into the dream, it had gone wherever dreams go, but I did manage to fall asleep again and got two more hours. Dreamless hours, as far as I could tell.

For breakfast I had a piece of toast and a cup of coffee, because in less than two hours I'd be meeting Ray Galindez for lunch at the Morning Star. It was getting on for noon when Elaine left for the Croatian church, and not long after that when I headed out for my meeting with Ray.

I picked a table at the front window where I could keep an eye on the door, and ordered coffee while I waited. I tried to remember the last time I'd seen

Ray, and I decided it had to be about as long ago as Ray Gruliow's last drink. Elaine had seen him more frequently than I, as they'd had an ongoing business relationship while her shop was still open. But as for me . . .

Maybe it had been longer than five years. Jesus, would I recognize him?

I kept looking toward the entrance, and it wasn't long before he came in, wearing pressed jeans and a blazer and carrying a black leather portfolio, and of course I recognized him instantly. I raised a hand, and he saw me and came over, and after the handshake he took a seat across from me.

"You look the same," I said.

"Is that a good thing or a bad thing? But you, Matt. You look terrific. What's so funny?"

"The three stages of a man's life," I said. "Youth, middle age, and 'You look wonderful!'"

"I never heard that one. But you do, you know. Life good?"

"No complaints."

"What about Elaine? Does she miss the shop?"

Once she'd left the life, Elaine looked around for something to do. She took classes and was a regular at her gym, but none of that was work, and she felt the need for work. She'd always had a good eye for art and antiques, and one day she signed a lease for a small Ninth Avenue storefront a few blocks south of our apartment. I forget what they used to sell there, but she replaced the existing sign with her name, ELAINE MARDELL, and stocked it with items from her storage locker.

One day we came home from a Matisse show at MOMA, and she said, "You know, he was a genius, and—"

"Matisse?"

"Uh-huh. A genius, and the Fauve style holds up marvelously, and I wouldn't want to say this in front of the man himself, or in front of anybody but you, actually, but—"

"But your average four-year-old kid could paint like that?"

"No," she said. "No no no. But there are some paintings of his that are not all that different from what you see in thrift shops. He knew what he was doing, and the thrift-shop artists didn't, except maybe intuitively. And he knew how to get the effects he wanted, and they didn't, and who's to say that they got what they were aiming for? But if you look through enough bins of amateur crap, like one thrift shop after another—"

"You might find something to hang on the walls."

"The shop's walls."

"Right."

"Not our walls."

"Perish the thought."

The shop was fun for her. Fun for both of us, in fact, as I sometimes spelled her when she had a yoga class or a hair appointment, or the urge to prowl second-hand shops in a search for the next unheralded masterpiece. I enjoyed the interaction with the people who wandered into the shop, didn't mind the bargaining that was a part of many transactions, and felt triumphant when somebody actually bought something.

The place showed a profit, although we would have been hard put to live on it. But it kept us busy and it earned its keep, and she'd still have it but for the fact that the landlord quadrupled the rent.

She came home and sat down with a pencil and paper, and an hour later she said she couldn't make it work. "We'd be losing minimum of two grand a month staying open," she said. "Probably more like three."

"We can do it if you want. We can afford it, can't we?"

She'd put money aside during her call girl years, then followed the advice of one of her regulars and began investing in real estate. Now she owned a batch of apartment houses in Queens, and enjoyed a nice stream of income from them. I had my pension and

Social Security, plus the occasional windfall dollars I'd managed to set aside, so we were comfortable. If we had to subsidize the shop to the tune of twenty-five or thirty thousand dollars a year, we could do so without missing any meals.

She shook her head. "It started out as a business. This would turn it into a hobby, and what the hell do I need with a hobby. You remember the joke?"

"The guy with the bees?"

"Thousand upon thousands of bees, and he lives in two rooms on Pitkin Avenue. 'Charlie, where do you keep them?' 'In a cigar box.' 'Don't they get all crushed, jammed together like that?' 'Hey, fuck it, it's only a hobby.' Well, I don't want a hobby."

AT THE MORNING STAR, I considered the question while the waitress came by and took our order. Then I said, "Does she miss it? Yes, I suppose she does. She never finds herself with time on her hands, she doesn't lack for things to do, but she took an empty storefront and turned it into a wonderful reflection of herself."

"Every square foot of it," he said, "was Elaine."

"And she got a kick out of finding something that nobody would look twice at and revealing it to be a work of art. One of her thrift shop specials turned out to be a Paint-by-Numbers masterpiece."

"She didn't spot that when she bought it?"

"She just liked the looks of it, and the Salvation Army wanted something like fifteen or twenty dollars for it, so she wasn't about to x-ray it. She bought it and brought it home. A week or so later a customer picked it up and said it looked to her like Paint-by-Numbers. Our girl didn't miss a beat. 'A perfect example of Outsider Art,' she said. 'This particular artist used Paint-by-Numbers as his jumping-off point. And do you see what he's done with it?'"

He nodded. "Anybody would miss moments like that," he said.

"She misses the action," I said, "and the stimulation. The give and take of it. Retail can be a nightmare, you're at the mercy of any ambulatory psychotic who walks in off the street, but she thrived on it. And once in a while she wound up working with a real artist."

"Jury's still out on that."

"Every time she sold a sketch of yours, and every time she got you a portrait commission, you'd think she'd just won the Nobel Prize. When she decided to close the shop, even before she told the landlord, she was looking for somebody to step up and rep you."

"I remember how I got the news. 'Ray, this is Johanna Huberman, she's got a small gallery on upper

Madison Avenue, and she'll be able to represent your work far better than I can. Oh, by the way, I've decided to close the shop.'"

"That sounds about right. Are you still with—"

"Johanna? I am, and Elaine chose well. We've got good chemistry. It's a slow way to get rich, but Jesus, Matt, I'm a professional artist. It's how I make my living. How the hell did that happen?"

WE SAT OVER COFFEE while I told him what he needed to know about Ellen. That didn't include her vocational history, or how Elaine happened to know her. They were in a group together, I said, and they'd gotten friendly over the months, and the younger woman had brought her problem to Elaine.

That problem, of course, was the putative Paul, who was transformed in the telling from a client of hers to a nut job who'd decided they were soulmates on the strength of a single dinner date. As far as she was concerned, one awkward evening was more than enough, but Paul didn't see it that way.

"So he's stalking her," he said.

"He's trying to. She moved out of her apartment, found another place to stay for the time being. She may have to change her phone number, but so far she hasn't."

"And he calls?"

"Early and often."

"She been to the police?"

"No, and I was going to send her there but I couldn't think what she could tell them. She doesn't know his last name, and she's not sure he gave her the right first name."

"Paul, you said."

"Right."

"Probably married," he said. "That'd explain not giving his real name. But that doesn't fit with the stalking, does it?"

"You wouldn't think so, but—"

"But maybe it does. If he's obsessed with her, all bets are off. There's a word for it."

"Stalking?"

"Erotomania. It's more than an obsession, it's the conviction that they've got a real relationship with the stalkee, if that's a word. Sometimes it's a public figure and they've never even met in real life. Like that woman they caught breaking into David Letterman's house."

"That was a while ago."

"Years," he said. "If she turned up again, I don't

know who she'd get fixated on. Colbert, I suppose. Or one of the Jimmies."

"Past my bedtime."

"Not me. I'm still a night owl, but I don't watch talk shows anymore. I have to say I miss David Letterman."

"You could always break into his house," I said. "He'd probably be happy to see you."

WHEN WE GOT TO the apartment, Ellen was sitting on the couch in the living room, her shoes off, wearing slacks and a sweater. I'd managed introductions by the time Elaine came in from the kitchen with a plate of shortbread cookies. Elaine told Ray how well he looked, and he told her she was as lovely as ever, and she put the plate of cookies on the coffee table, where no one paid any attention to them. Elaine told Ellen it had been worth running the shop just to be able to offer Ray's work, and Ray told Ellen how Elaine had discovered him. "But it wasn't like discovering America," he said, "or a new planet."

Elaine told him he was modest to a fault, and he said he had a lot to be modest about, and then the air went out of the small talk. Ray unzipped his portfolio and took out a sketch pad and a pencil case, and Elaine said, "Well, you two have work to do. The light's better in the front room."

When they were out of range, she said, "I hope this works. She didn't want to come."

"Why not?"

"She's afraid it won't work. And it'll be her fault."

'It'll probably work just fine."

"I know."

"And it won't be anybody's fault if it doesn't."

"I know that, too. Nobody touched the cookies."

"Until now," I said, and ate one.

"I don't know why I feel compelled to do that."

"Bring out food?"

"It's the most Jewish thing about me. What?"

" 'What?' "

"You were about to say something."

I took another cookie. "These don't taste particularly Jewish," I said.

"They're from Pepperidge Fucking Farm, and that's not what you were about to say."

"Can you think of anything I could possibly say that wouldn't come off as either anti-Semitic or misogynistic?"

"Not offhand," she said.

―〽―

....

I COULDN'T TELL YOU when I met Ray Galindez, but I can picture him that first time, sitting at a desk in a station house, a sketch pad in one hand and a pencil in the other. Early in his career with the NYPD, he'd revealed a special talent for working with witnesses and translating their memories into detailed drawings. A lot of police artists use some version of IdentiKit, swapping eyes and lips and jawlines back and forth, until the witness is happy with the result, and there are times when that works pretty well. It's better a lot of the time than the old-fashioned you-talk-and-I-draw method, because there aren't all that many talented artists in blue uniforms, while just about anyone can learn how to rock an IdentiKit.

But nobody with an IdentiKit could come anywhere near Ray Galindez.

It wasn't just that he was a very capable sketch artist. If you keep your eyes open you'll see a lot of men and women with pencils and sketch books, in subway cars or coffee shops or public parks, sneaking peeks at someone across the way and trying to summon up a likeness. Sometimes I'd sneak a peek of my own, at the emerging sketch, and while there was something wrong with most of the drawings, on balance they were surprisingly good. *Yes*, you'd think, *that's her, all right. There's something not quite right about the mouth, but it's not bad.*

....

But they had an advantage. They were able to see the person they were attempting to draw.

All Ray had was witnesses armed with whatever lingered in their visual memory. To get that down on paper, he had to coax that memory back to life and draw what it gave him. He had to be sensitive to the witnesses he worked with, and intuitive enough to sense what it meant when one of them said, "No, his eyebrows were angrier than that. Meaner."

Some years ago, I'd spent a fair amount of time with a resourceful serial murderer. At the time, I thought of him as a drunk trying to get sober, and a possible future friend—which is to say that he played me very effectively. When the penny dropped, I sat down with Ray and it didn't take him long to get my false friend's likeness on his pad, and I printed a ton of copies and flooded the city with them.

That was relatively easy, because I had a strong visual impression of the man, and could look at his sketch pad and say what did or did not match up to the image in my mind. But Ray had the uncanny ability to draw upon memories that were hazy at best, childhood recollections with the subject's features worn away by the years. Elaine first discovered this when she got him to draw a relative she barely remembered, a man whose face she could not manage to picture in her mind.

She framed the result, and gave it a prominent spot in her shop, with a NOT FOR SALE tag on it. Before long she was lining up commissions for Ray, matching him with a woman whose only photo of her long-dead father had been lost in a fire. Word of mouth brought more work, including a tour de force for a Holocaust survivor, for which he dredged out memories of all her dead relatives and sketched them seated together at a dinner table.

According to Elaine, it came out looking like a cross between a Seder in Lithuania and Leonardo's *The Last Supper*. "To Mrs. Reisman," she said, "all it looked like was family. First she couldn't stop crying, and then she couldn't stop kissing Ray's hands."

ELAINE RETURNED TO A novel she was trying to finish, and I had another go at the *Times*, and I was getting bad news from the Science section about the prospects of polar bears, when Ray and Ellen joined us after a half hour or so. She wasn't kissing his hands, but then again he hadn't just drawn a face she longed to remember. The man who looked up from Ray's sketch pad was one she'd have preferred to forget.

I couldn't judge the extent to which the drawing did or did not capture its subject. I'd never laid eyes on Paul, and had no better idea of what he looked like than I had of his actual name. The face I saw was a wide-browed oval, the eyes deep-set, the lips full, the jawline the least bit jowly. There was menace in the subject's gaze, resolve in the set of his mouth and jaw, and no way to know how much of that was real and how much the emotional baggage Ellen brought to the table.

But the result was the specific portrait of a specific person. IdentiKit compilations have always reminded me of Mr. Potato Head, and like most police sketches they're a little less than the sum of their parts. This, on the other hand, appeared to have been drawn from life.

"It's him," Ellen said.

RAY WOULDN'T TAKE ANY money, not even for expenses. He said, "What, subway fare? Come on."

But he couldn't escape without a Tupperware container filled with the rest of the shortbread cookies. "Otherwise Matt will eat them," Elaine told him, "and he's already had more than he should."

"Well, in that case," Ray said.

After he'd left, Ellen hung around long enough to eat a sandwich and marvel at how easy it had been to work with Ray, how it was like he was reading her mind with his pencil. Elaine took her downstairs, stopping three doors down to make half a dozen photocopies of Ray's work. One was for Ellen, whom she then tucked into a cab, after first scanning the sidewalks for the man in the sketch.

"At least this time I knew what I was looking for," she said. By then she'd laid out the copies and Ray's original on the coffee table, regarding each in turn as if to assess the consistency of the Xerox machine. After a moment she took the original into another room, where it would bide its time until it reached Johanna Huberman's hands. Ideally it would wind up sharing a mat and frame with a mug shot of its subject.

"He's really remarkable," she said of Ray, and I pointed out that we wouldn't really know how remarkable he was until we got our own look at the stalker. "According to Ellen," she said, "it's the spitting image. Where does that expression come from, anyway?"

"I have no idea."

"And I don't really care. There should be a word for apathy so profound that you don't even bother Googling it."

"There probably is."

"But in order to know that word," she said, "you'd

have to . . . Never mind. I'm glad he took the cookies. They were good, weren't they?"

"I don't suppose one or two wouldn't fit in the container."

"No, they fit perfectly."

"Next time," I said, "use a smaller container."

"He gave up the better part of a day," she said, "and schlepped all the way in from Williamsburg—"

"It's not that much of a schlep."

"—and you begrudge the man a handful of shortbread cookies."

"Who knows if he even likes shortbread?"

"Everybody likes shortbread."

I said, "I was just thinking that he might have been just as happy with a little cupcake."

"A wee bit of crumpet to go with his tea?" She considered this. "I never saw Ray as a man with a roving eye. He's crazy about Bitsy. Or at least he used to be."

"Still is."

"Of course," she said, "one can never lose sight of the fact that all men are swine." She thought for a moment. "What did you pick up? Was she encouraging him?"

"She put her hand on top of his."

"When?"

"While you were packing up his cookies. They were sitting side by side—"

"On the couch."

"—and his hand was on the table, palm down, and she said something and used her hands for emphasis."

"She does that."

"Most people do. And when she finished what she was saying, she put her hand on top of his."

"What, like this?" Her hand covered mine.

"Like that."

"Or was it more like this?"

Her hand pressed down a little on mine, and I felt a transfer of energy.

"Jesus," I said.

"You don't forget how," she mused. "Even after all these years, even if life has turned you into an old married lady, you still remember the moves. And our Ellen's neither old nor married, and she's been out of the game for what, about a minute and a half? Did he get the message?"

"His eyes widened a little bit."

"With surprise?"

I thought about it. "No."

"No, because he wasn't surprised. Because she would have done a little of the touchy-feely when they were in front working on the sketch. But he'd see that as unconscious, part of being caught up in the process. It'd be enough to get him thinking of her in sexual terms, just in a very surfacey way, but that's all."

"And then she did it again, after their work was done. And this time she did it with an audience."

"She did it in front of you," she said. "But not in front of me."

"Because you'd be more likely to pick up on it."

"And because I'm her sponsor, or the next thing to it, and she didn't want me to catch her acting like a whore."

"You really think that's what she was doing?"

"Oh, no question. A refined whore, though. I mean, what did she do? Touch the back of his hand? It's not as if she grabbed him by the dick."

AN HOUR LATER, AFTER I'd put in some time at the computer while she returned to her novel, it occurred to me to wonder why.

"Why touch his hand? To get him interested."

"Obviously," I said, "but why? You think she wants to go to bed with him?"

"I'm pretty sure she doesn't." She marked her place, closed her book. "Part of it's reflex," she said.

"Even before she started turning tricks, probably long before it ever occurred to her, she learned how to relate to guys."

"Touch their hands."

"Get them interested," she said. "Touching is one way to do that."

"So that's all it is?"

She shook her head. "She'd want him to like her. She'd want him on her side. He came here to do us a favor, but he was also doing her a favor, and he might do a better job or go an extra mile if he liked her."

"And would he?"

"Not consciously," she said, "but sure. Didn't you extend yourself more for the clients you liked? I don't mean sexually. You liked some of the people you worked for more than some of the others."

"Early on," I remembered, "I preferred to work for clients I didn't like. Because it wouldn't bother me as much to disappoint them. But I guess you're right. You work harder for the ones you like."

"It's only natural."

And, I wondered, had she herself worked harder to please some johns than others? Slipped with them into a deeper level of intimacy? Played her part with more enthusiasm? Held in reserve certain acts she'd only perform with the chosen ones?

I didn't ask. I could have, and if the matter

obsessed me I probably would have, but I didn't feel the need. The years she'd spent in the profession had been a natural outgrowth of the girl she'd been, even as they'd since become a part of who she was now.

I said, "I can see her wanting to motivate him with a little intimacy. But afterward the sketch was finished and he was on his way home to wife and children—"

"A reward for a job well done."

"Oh."

"And to show that she still liked him even after there was no longer anything to get from him. And I was out of the room."

"While I'd never notice."

"Sure you would. You're a detective, you're observant by nature. And if you noticed, that was all to the good. Because it gave her a chance to flirt with you at one remove. 'I'm a kind of a sexy lady, and I like guys, and if the circumstances were right it'd be your hand I was touching.'"

I didn't say anything, and I guess I was looking off into the middle distance, because she said, "What?"

"I was thinking of the little fantasy we shared yesterday."

"The two-person threesome? Now there's a surprise. Whoever could have guessed you'd think of that? And what exactly were you thinking?"

"That she didn't have to prove anything to me. That I already knew she was a sexy lady, because I remembered all the stuff she did with such enthusiasm. And then I had to remind myself that she hadn't done anything because she wasn't even in the room."

AT THE BREAKFAST TABLE the next morning Elaine announced that she was on her way to a yoga class. Did she look all right?

She was wearing a tailored jacket in Black Watch plaid over a blue silk top and a pair of black jeans.

I said, "For yoga class? That's a big step up from baggy sweat pants and a Mötley Crüe T-shirt."

She held up her gym bag, a carry-on from a defunct airline. "Sweats and a top," she said. "They're not that baggy."

"Okay."

"And I don't even own a Mötley Crüe shirt. The closest I come is The Bad Plus T-shirt you insisted on buying for me when we saw them at the Vanguard. And it's in the wash."

"Whatever you say."

"After yoga," she said, "I have to meet with a priest."

"If you actually confess everything—"

"A Croatian priest."

"Oh."

"What we decided at yesterday's meeting," she said, "is our Tuesday noon meeting isn't enough. We'd like to schedule an evening meeting."

"In the same church."

"If they've got the space available. We're trying for Fridays, but we'll take Thursdays if we have to."

"Friday would be good," I said.

"Not too close to Tuesday. Plus from a purely self-ish point of view, that's when you've got your regular meeting at St. Paul's."

"Two birds," I said.

"Well, a bird for each of us. So that'd be two birds and two stones. I'll have an hour between yoga and when I'm supposed to meet Marjorie on the corner. Then we walk to the church and meet with Father Tomislav. And then we'll probably have lunch. I'll let you know if I'm going to be late." She made a face. "You know what? This blouse is wrong."

"What's the matter with it?"

"It's too blue," she said, "and too clingy."

She went to change and I took what was left of my coffee into the living room. I was looking at Ray's sketch of Ellen's stalker—a photocopy, the original pencil sketch was safely tucked away—when she returned, the blue silk blouse replaced by an Oxford cloth shirt with a button-down collar.

"Still blue," I pointed out.

"But not too blue. Do I look okay?"

"To meet a priest? Perfect, I'd say. You look like an altar boy."

SHE LEFT, AND HALF an hour later so did I. It had rained some during the night, but now the sun was out. I caught the southbound One train at Columbus Circle and got off at Twenty-Eighth Street and Seventh Avenue. That put me just one block north of Ellen's apartment, but a good half-mile west of it.

I took my time walking across town. I couldn't remember the last time I'd been in that part of the city, and for years I'd taken pride in how well I knew the town, how frequently I walked its streets. Not too many years ago, unless I was in a hurry I might have skipped the subway and walked the whole way. A couple of miles on a perfect fall morning? Why not?

Well, my knee was one answer to that question, but not the only one. It would take me longer these days, because my pace is slower than it used to be. And it would take energy, of which I seem to have a finite supply. I'd find places to stop along the way. A bench in Bryant Park, if my route took me there. A coffee shop, a pizza stand.

And I wasn't just taking the air, or walking for exercise, or killing time. I had a job to do. I had a client, I was working.

Or going through the motions. Sometimes it's hard to tell.

UNTIL SHE FLED, FIRST to a hotel and then to an Upper West Side sublet, Ellen Lipscomb had lived in a six-story limestone-front building on the south side of East 27th Street between Third and Lexington. The front door was up a half-flight of concrete steps, and opened into a vestibule. I went in and had a look at the double column of buttons on my left. Each had a slot next to it for the tenant's name. Three or four of them had elected to remain anonymous, while the rest ranged from embossed labels available from locksmith shops to printed names cut from business cards, all the way down to hand-lettered scraps of paper like the one next to button 4-B. No first name, not even an initial: LIPSCOMB.

I rang the bell. I didn't expect a response, and didn't get one. I counted buttons and did the math, and determined what I'd already suspected: that there were four apartments to a floor. 4-B would be either right front or left rear.

The label for the twenty-fifth bell, at the very bottom of the second column, was professionally made. It read SUPERINTENDANT, which looked wrong, but if you look at any word long enough it looks to be misspelled. I let my finger hover over the button, then withdrew it.

Outside, I walked the rest of the way to Third Avenue, crossed to the north side, and walked back to Cuppa, a non-Starbucks coffee bar I'd noticed earlier. There were three tables opposite the service counter, two empty and the third occupied by a young woman typing furiously on a laptop. There was also a butcher-block counter in the front window, with three unoccupied stools. I got a small black coffee from the mixed-race barista. A Vietnamese mother, I decided, and an African-American serviceman father. I carried my coffee to the counter in front, picked the stool farthest to the right, because that gave me the best view of Ellen's building, though I'd have been hard put to tell you why I felt the need to gaze at it.

I decided it was probably sexist or racist or something of the sort to assume it was the mother who was Vietnamese, the father a black American. I ran possibilities through my mind, and I got as far as anyone could without sending the young woman's DNA to a lab, and at that point I asked myself what the hell I thought I was doing.

I took out my phone. No texts, no messages. I opened the Google app and typed in *superintendant,* and Google confirmed what I'd suspected, that the correct spelling was *superintendent.* Then I typed in *attendent,* which didn't look right, and it wasn't. *Attendant,* Google told me.

How the hell is anyone supposed to learn this fucking language?

I TOOK OUT THE sketch, looked at it. Looked out the window, as if the son of a bitch would be there to be seen, skulking in doorways and eyeballing her building.

When I got to the bottom of my cup of coffee, I quit stalling. I showed the sketch to the barista, who wanted to know who he was and what he'd done. "We've had reports," I said.

"Reports?"

"Complaints, you might say."

She hadn't seen him. I handed her a card, one that had only my name and cellphone number on it. Would she take another look at the sketch, just to fix it in her mind? And would she call me if she saw him?

The woman with the laptop had curly red hair and a pointed chin. She also had a lot of questions: Who was he? What had he done? And who was I, and what was my interest in the matter? He'd been bothering women, I admitted, and there was a good possibility he was dangerous.

"Well, I'm not afraid of him," she said. She took my card, promised she'd call.

I WORKED BOTH SIDES of the block, stopped in every commercial establishment. A dry cleaner, an Indo-Pak grocery, a bodega, a wine bar. At a corner diner, the cashier said he looked familiar, but she saw hundreds of people every day, and they all looked familiar. The counterman looked at the sketch, frowned, and said, "Oh, sure."

"You know him?"

"I'm good at faces. Ask anybody."

"I'll take your word for it. When did you see him?"

"Dates and times," he said, "I ain't so good at. He was here twice, sat on that stool one time and that one the other. Or maybe it was the other way around."

"But you don't know when this was."

"Well, I come on at noon, and I'm out of here by ten. As far as when, I'd say within the past week or so. Wasn't today, wasn't yesterday. I'm not much help, am I?"

"You're doing okay."

"I can tell you what he ordered," he said. "Same thing both times. A tuna melt and well-done fries. That help?"

I KNEW WHAT TO do. And I knew I was stalling, because I was an old man with a bad knee and all I was fit for these days was thinking of things for other people to do.

Back in the day, I'd have given a copy of the sketch to TJ and posted him where he could keep an eye on Ellen's building. When I'd chummed the waters enough to draw Paul, TJ could have followed him, learned who he was and where he lived and worked.

Then I could have set the hook and reeled him in.

Back in the day, once he was in the boat, once I'd landed him, I'd have had Mick with me to use the muscle I'd let go soft—and the mental resolve, which had just as irreversibly gone to fat.

Back in the day.

But that was then and this was now, and I could see what I had to do, and that I had to do it all by myself.

BACK AT ELLEN'S BUILDING, I entered the vestibule and rang the super's bell. I was about to ring it again when a voice over the intercom fought its way through the static to ask who I was and what I wanted. I matched the static myself with a garbled response that included the words *your tenant* and *police matter*. It was a legal way to say something without saying anything, and it drew in response a heavy sigh—clear as a bell, static or no—and, a beat later, "Be right up."

A few minutes later he stepped through the door to join me in the vestibule. He was a black man, and I thought immediately of the barista and wondered if he'd left a Vietnamese wife in their basement apartment.

But he wasn't old enough for Vietnam. He was around fifty, maybe fifty-five, my height, and he was balding and beginning to show the years. He was wearing medium-gray coveralls, and he had big shoulders, but he also had a gut on him, too, and the way he moved suggested this was a recent addition and he couldn't figure out where it could have come from.

I showed him Ray's sketch, asked him if he'd seen its subject.

He took a long thoughtful look, then shook his head. "Never seen him," he said.

"You're sure of that?"

"Absolutely."

Good. I'd known halfway through the long look that he'd lie about it, and that *Absolutely* of his sealed the deal. *"Mr. Simpson, how do you plead to the homicide charges?" "Absolutely positively one hundred percent not guilty."*

Right.

So he had something to lie about, and he was no good at lying. I couldn't have had better news.

"Take another look," I suggested. "It's evident that he came here within the past few days asking about a tenant of yours."

"I would remember," he said.

"And I think you will, when I tell you the tenant in question was a young woman named Ellen Lipscomb."

"I think she moved out."

"Oh?"

"Her rent's paid through the first of the month, so no problem, but I haven't seen her in a while."

"Why does that make you think she moved out?"

"Well, you know—"

"What happens when one of your tenants flies home to Ohio for Thanksgiving? Or heads out to the Hamptons for a week? Do you call the landlord, tell him to list the apartment?"

He let out a sigh a few pounds heavier than the one that had come through the intercom. "Oh, sweet Jesus," he said. "Is she all right? Miss Lipscomb?"

"What makes you ask?"

"You, you're what makes me ask. Showing me that picture." He reached out, moved the sketch to see it better. "Is this a photograph? It looks like a drawing."

"It's a photocopy of a portrait," I said, truthfully enough. "And you recognize it, don't you?"

"It's her brother."

I didn't say anything.

"That's what he said. He was her brother, she'd gone missing, the family was worried about her. He's not her brother, is he?"

"Not even close."

"Did he—"

"What?"

"Hurt her?"

"Not yet," I said.

I watched as pain and fear came into his eyes.

Showing, not for the first time, that a bad liar is often a good man.

"He said he was her brother, her older brother, and he said he was working with the police. But both of those things—"

"Weren't true."

"He said she had a mental condition, that's what he called it, a condition. And that was why she saw men for money. That part's true, isn't it?"

"That she had a mental condition?"

"That she saw men for money. I got that impression, the visitors I'd see coming down from her apartment. And Christmas."

"Christmas?"

"The tips she'd give me," he said, "were the highest of anybody in the building. Everybody knows working girls are the best tippers."

"Let's get back to our friend here," I said. "How'd he find you?"

"He rang the bell. I came upstairs. He wasn't out here, he was in the hallway. Either he had a key or somebody held the door for him. They're not supposed to do that, but it's human, you know? You don't want to insult a man by shutting the door in his face. And he was dressed nice, suit and tie."

"So he didn't look like a junkie, there to steal a TV set."

"No, he looked respectable."

"You never saw him before?"

"When would I see him? Oh, he was here before? He was her—"

"Client, yes."

"My God," he said. "I let him into her apartment. I waited for him while he went around, opening drawers, touching her things." He looked at me. "He acted like he had the right. Do you know what I mean?"

I nodded.

"And he gave me money. Not like, 'Here's a hundred bucks if you'll let me into her apartment.' More like the family wanted him to check on her, because of her situation, and taking his wallet out of his breast pocket while he's talking, and he takes out the bill and folds it and says, 'Something for your trouble,' and tucks it into my hand."

Yes, that would be how he would do it.

"Did he say his name?"

"Lipscomb, the same as hers. But if he wasn't her brother—"

"Then his name probably wasn't Lipscomb. No first name?"

"I can't remember."

"He would have wanted you to get in touch with him," I suggested. "To let him know if she came back."

"He had this little notebook, wrote something and

folded it and slipped it into my palm the same way he gave me the money for my troubles." He frowned at the phrase. "A name and a phone number. I thought, *No, sir. I'm not about to call you.*"

"This was after he'd been in her apartment."

He nodded. "I stayed there, and we walked out together, and I locked up. And then he gave me that slip of paper."

"You still have it?"

"No way I was gonna call that man."

"But you kept the paper."

"I believe I've still got it. If I threw it out I'd remember, wouldn't I?"

WE WALKED THE LENGTH of the hallway and took the flight of stairs that led down into the basement. Because the first floor was half a flight up from sidewalk level, the basement got a certain amount of light from the street. He was evidently a good super, he kept it neat, and his apartment was a comfortable one, and nicely furnished.

In my experience, superintendents generally had decent furniture. Tenants moved out and left things, and the supers got first choice.

If there was a wife in the apartment, Vietnamese

or otherwise, she kept out of sight and silent. But his place looked like that of a neat man who lived alone. He offered me a chair, which I didn't take, and asked if I wanted a glass of water or something. I said I was fine.

"It's here somewhere," he said, as if unsure exactly where, and then went unerringly to a desk, opened the top drawer on the right, and drew out a folded 3x5 sheet of ruled paper. He opened it, gave it a quick read, then refolded it and handed it to me.

Paul Lipscomb, I read, and a phone number.

It couldn't be that easy, I thought, and I drew out my own notebook and found the right page. If he'd given the super his home number, or the number of his personal cell phone, then I had him. Five minutes in front of my computer and I'd know everything I needed to know about the son of a bitch.

But, as it turned out, it really couldn't be that easy. The number he'd written down, next to the name that wasn't his, was in fact the same burner he'd used for his calls to Ellen.

I folded the slip and found a spot for it in my wallet. He looked as though he might have wanted it back, but didn't know how to ask for it.

I said, "You won't be calling him."

"Of course not. Can I ask you something? Did you used to be a cop?"

"Years ago."

"Thought so. You got the manner, but—"

"But I'm a few years past retirement age. I'm working private now." I found a business card. "Matthew Scudder," I said.

He repeated my name, told me his was Henry Loudon. I wrote that down, and asked him his phone number, and wrote that down, too. "He might call," I said.

"He hasn't so far," he said. "If he does, well, any number I don't know pops up, I let it go straight to voice mail."

"It's also possible he'll show up."

"That man rings my buzzer, I'm in the middle of a furnace repair."

"Good," I said, and got out my own wallet, and found a hundred-dollar bill of my own. He didn't want to take it, insisted it wasn't necessary.

I insisted it was, told him he'd helped me and saved me a lot of time. And that he had my card, and if our friend got in touch, I wanted him to let me know right away.

"I'd do that anyway," he said. "When you showed me his picture, you know I recognized that man right away."

"I got that impression."

"Why I lied about it, I was ashamed of myself.

Taking that man's money, letting that man into her apartment."

"You thought he was her brother."

"Not by the end of it I didn't. You know what he did?"

Went in the closet, I thought, and had a look at her alligator handbag.

"I said he touched her things."

"Yes, you told me."

"Almost like he was touching her, and not like a brother. And you know what else? He went into the bathroom."

"Oh?"

"She has this clothes hamper. Wicker, you know? He screened it with his body, so I wouldn't see, and then he lifted the lid and reached in and fumbled around with her dirty clothes. Took something out."

I waited.

"Panties, I think. Didn't get a good look, didn't want to get a good look, but I think it was panties. Panties from the dirty clothes." He took a deep breath. "So that's why I acted like I didn't recognize him." He corrected himself. "Why I *told* you I didn't recognize him. On account of I wanted to put all of that out of mind."

I laid a hand on his shoulder. "No worries, Henry," I said. "It's all going to work out."

‒‒‒‒‒

PANTIES.

Not a good sign.

I WAS SITTING AT the computer when Elaine came in, pleased to report that Father Tomislav would be happy to rent out the basement room for a second meeting. Fridays wouldn't work, but they could have it every Thursday evening from 7:30 to 9.

"Then Marjorie and I had lunch, and then we went to her place and called everybody to let them know we'd be having a meeting tomorrow night. He's nice."

"Father Tomislav?"

"I'm not sure who he thinks we are."

"You didn't tell him the group name was the Tarts?"

"I said we were affiliated with Working Women of America."

"Is that a thing?"

"It would have almost to be, don't you think? I probably could have said Working Girls of America, he seems too innocent to be familiar with the term."

"Or it'll remind him of the Meg Ryan movie."

"Melanie Griffith," she said gently. "I think I gave him the impression that it's like AA for women who work for a living. Which isn't that far from the truth, is it? And how was your day?"

I told her, and she complimented me on having accomplished so much, and I moved a hand to wave the words aside. "I did everything wrong," I told her. "Sit on your ass for a few years and your instincts go south. I got most of my way through the conversation with the super before I remembered to ask his name, or tell him mine."

"You should have done that right away?"

"Of course, and it should have been automatic. I should have asked Henry to let me into the apartment, so that he could have seen me do nothing but look around. That would let him decide it was okay for me to be there."

"But you didn't ask?"

"He asked me," I said, "if I wanted to go upstairs, and I said there was no need. As soon as the words were out of my mouth I wanted to change my mind, but the timing would have been off. Jesus, I hope he didn't call Paul's burner phone five minutes after I left."

"You think it's possible?"

"I took the number with me, but he could have

copied it down somewhere. Or even memorized it." I thought about it. "No," I said. "I don't think he made the call. I think he knew beyond question that Paul—I wish I had something else to call the son of a bitch."

"Mr. Lipscomb?"

"Yeah, right. He knew it wasn't her older brother. And that means he'd been lied to, and tricked, and a hundred bucks wasn't adequate compensation for that."

"And you'd matched the hundred, sort of canceling it out."

"But you know what really did it?"

"The panties?"

"Far as Henry's concerned, that makes him a pervert. And that's good, but it's also not so good."

"Oh?"

"He's dangerous," I said.

"Didn't we know that?"

"Stealing her soiled panties," I said, "right out of the hamper, with every chance he'd be observed doing so."

"Purposely tempting fate?"

"More like too obsessed to hold himself in check. We knew he was dangerous," I said. "We just didn't know how dangerous."

· ·

—*mm*—

AGES AGO, WHEN THEY swore me in as a NYPD cop, I wore a uniform I'd bought at Jonas Rathburn & Sons, a cop shop around the corner from the old Centre Street headquarters. Over the years I picked up other gear there—handcuffs, a Kevlar vest, a nightstick to replace the one that disappeared one whiskey-soaked evening. Rathburn stayed put when the department relocated at One Police Plaza, which was around the time that I ended my first marriage and my first career, moving from a house in Syosset to a hotel room on West 57th Street, turning in my service revolver and my shield.

It was a gold shield by then—I'd made detective some years before the day when I realized that I was done being a husband, just as I was done being a cop. So I hadn't worn the blue uniform in a long time. I'd packed it up, along with the gear a detective had no use for, and we stored it in the basement.

I was a few years out of the marriage and out of Syosset when Anita called to tell me a pipe had broken in the basement, and the consequent flooding had soaked my uniform and whatever else was in the carton. What did I want her to do with it?

I was surprised she still had it. Throw it out, I said. All of it? All of it.

· ·

So Thursday morning, after a night of running scenarios in my mind, I took a train downtown and found my way to The Police Building, which was the name a developer had fastened on the Beaux Arts building on Centre Street, after he'd converted it for residential use. I walked around the corner to where Rathburn & Sons had always been, and their storefront was now a Starbucks.

Nobody remembered that particular cop shop, including Google. It took me ten or fifteen minutes to walk to One Police Plaza, and I spent most of that time wondering what had led me to assume Rathburn would still be around, doing business in the same old location.

On Madison Street, I spotted a shop with a big poster in the window, Jerry Orbach as Lennie Briscoe. I went in and found where they kept the batons, picked one up, and remembered the comfort mine had provided in my early days in uniform. I'd had a .38 on my hip, a more formidable weapon than any nightstick could possibly be, but I thought of it just for show. The last thing I wanted was to have to yank it out of its holster.

I found one that had a nice balance to it and took it to the counter. The man behind it, who'd shaved his head to hide a bald spot, asked if I was on the job.

"Years ago," I said, and smiled. "So I'm afraid I'm no longer eligible for the discount."

"You're not even eligible to pay full price," he told me. "Police baton's classified as a deadly weapon."

Which meant he couldn't sell it to anyone but a working police officer. I was trying to make sense out of this when he told me he bet he knew why I wanted it.

"Amateur theater," he said. "You're in a play, they've got you playing a cop, and since you used to be one it's good casting. Am I right?"

"That's it," I said.

"You rented a uniform at a costume shop, or maybe you can still fit into the one you wore on the job, in which case congratulations. But what you want is one of these, and the law won't let me sell it to you. That about right?"

"How'd you know?"

"Not because I'm psychic. I won't say I get this all the time, but you're not the first person ever came in here looking for a prop. I can help you out. Give me a minute."

He went in back, came out carrying a nightstick, slapping it gently against his palm. It was a twin to the one I'd picked out, and from his smile I guess my puzzlement must have shown on my face. "Here," he said, and began to hand it to me, then yanked it back and smacked himself full force on the crown of his hairless head.

BALSA, OF COURSE, AS he explained when he finally stopped laughing at the look on my face. Perfect for film or theater, looked just like the real thing, and cheap enough to smash one over somebody's head in every performance or dress rehearsal. Twelve bucks, and an NYPD-approved baton was over a hundred when you added on the sales tax. So how many would I like?

I said I'd have to check first with the director.

YOU COULD GO ONLINE and order a dozen different kinds of ninja shit, blowguns and throwing stars and nunchucks and other things I don't know the name of. You could walk into a gun show and walk out with an AR-15 and mow down a few dozen schoolkids. In those states with a righteous commitment to the Second Amendment, you could get yourself a mortar and a bazooka and, if you had the place to park it, a fucking cannon.

But if you were in New York City and you couldn't

show NYPD identification, they wouldn't let you get your hands on an overpriced wooden stick.

I walked around for a few minutes, picked up a cup of coffee at a hole in the wall called Joe-2-Go, sat on a bench in a pocket park long enough to drink it.

It didn't have to be a nightstick, I decided, or a sap, or anything else that the local authorities didn't want me to have. What it did have to be was something I could buy that very day, over the counter and for cash.

I used my phone's MapQuest app to orient me, tossed my Joe-2-Go cup in the trash, and followed the suggested route to the Bowery.

IT USED TO BE all flophouses and bars. The bars were dives, but of a different order of magnitude from what nowadays get called *dive bars*. The term of choice back then was *bucket of blood*, and it fit.

The flophouses were a warren of cubicles, each just large enough to accommodate a cot. They were separated from one another by partitions, their lower halves wallboard, topped with chicken wire reaching to the ceiling. The cacophony and the odor and the lack of privacy were enough to make real sleep impossible, even for men unaccustomed to quiet or fresh air or a private life. You had to be drunk enough to pass out, and when they woke you for early morning checkout, it didn't break your heart to get out of there.

I never got down that far, and my personal history is such that I doubt it would ever have happened; I'd have been safely dead of an alcohol-induced seizure before I got all that close to the Bowery. But in various storefronts and church basements I'd heard the stories of men who'd put in their time in those bars and flophouses, or lit fires in trash cans for warmth and warmed themselves more with Night Train or Thunderbird. Some of them got sober and some of them stayed sober, and one who'd reached the early stages of Korsakoff's syndrome, with swiss-cheese holes in his brain, had somehow wound up managing a 54-bed rehab facility in New Jersey, just outside of Trenton.

The job had taken me in and out of flophouses. That was back in my uniformed days, and I went there with a partner when a desk clerk called the precinct house to report a death. Sometimes the clerk didn't find the body right away, or delayed making the call, and on such occasions the smell was even worse than the usual flophouse stench. But it was always awful.

I'd been in a bucket of blood a handful of times, on occasions when they lived up to their name. An argument got out of hand, and one man hit another with a bottle or stabbed him with a knife. When you had to deal with something like that you needed a drink, but I never needed one badly enough to have it on the premises.

Of course a lot of Bowery habitués stayed out of the flophouses and passed out on the sidewalk, and that was a better idea in the warmer months. During the winter, a van made the rounds first thing in the morning, and anybody who still had a pulse would be hauled off to the drunk tank, because there was no such thing as detox then, not unless you were somebody rich drying out in Connecticut.

Then a second van would pick up the dead ones, and their next stop was Potter's Field.

That was then. Now the Bowery is a prestige address, with artists' lofts that artists can no longer afford, and condominiums built for absentee Russian oligarchs. I walked past designer boutiques and other hallmarks of over-the-top gentrification, but what the Bowery had the most of was establishments dealing in kitchen supplies, wholesalers who did a retail business as well.

I tossed a mental coin, walked into a shop named Edvard Magnusson, who must have been the firm's founder or proprietor. I browsed, and a helpful clerk turned up to show me variations on a theme. I made my selection and paid for it in cash.

I'd been keeping an eye open for a sporting goods store, but if I passed one I never spotted it. I remembered that there was a big one on my way, but I couldn't recollect the name and wasn't sure about the address.

I hauled out my phone and let Yelp tell me I was thinking of Paragon, at 18th and Broadway.

It was a long walk, but a nice day for it. Paragon was right where my phone had told me it would be, and I didn't need a clerk's help to find what I was looking for. I was waiting to pay for it when I noticed a kid with a backpack, and I gave up my place in the checkout line and found one for myself—small, navy blue, inexpensive and anonymous.

I got back in line, paid cash, and walked out with a Paragon shopping bag to go with the one from Edvard Magnusson.

Nobody at either place of business asked me to prove I was a cop. They just rang up the sales and let it go at that.

I WALKED ON, HEADING uptown. Along the way I realized I was hungry, and got a strong sudden urge for a tuna melt. I knew right where to get one, with a side of well-done fries, but decided that would be stupid. I didn't need to renew my acquaintance with that counterman, the one who never forgot a face or a food order.

New York diners, with breakfast served all day long and menus the size of phone books, had become an endangered species. Most had been done in by rent increases, like so many of the shops that made the city a joy to explore; some had gone out of business when the sons or grandsons of the Greek immigrants who'd started them decided there had to be an easier way to make a better living. I walked clear over to Second Avenue without finding one, and by then the curious yen for a tuna melt had dissipated. I ducked into a Thai restaurant and would have asked the waitress to confirm that the Drunken Noodles didn't contain any alcohol, then realized I wouldn't take her word for it anyway and said I'd have a plate of Pad Thai.

After I'd ordered, I took my shopping bags to the bathroom, where I locked myself in and did some consolidation, tucking two of my purchases into the third. I shouldered the backpack, got rid of the shopping bags, and wasted a few moments hand-shredding the receipts and flushing them down the commode.

Silly, I thought. Passing up the tuna melt from Mr. Memory was at least marginally sensible, but this was not.

And it was not as though I'd need the receipts for tax purposes. The JanSport backpack was under $25, and it was the most expensive item of the lot.

I PUT THE BACKPACK on the floor next to me while I ate my Pad Thai and drank a Thai coffee, which was essentially a milkshake with caffeine. I paid cash for my meal—it was good I'd hit an ATM early on, as I was paying cash for everything—and donned the backpack. I started out with it centered on my back with an arm through each of the straps, and then I shifted it to my right shoulder, and then to my left shoulder.

I felt about the way I'd feel if I bought a baseball cap and wore it backwards. Just as well I didn't have that far to go.

I FOUND A PLACE to stand across the street from Ellen's building. I stayed put for a full ten minutes, during which time nobody came in or out, and no lights went on in what might have been her apartment. I hadn't thought to ask Henry about the floor plan, and didn't suppose it mattered, but it was another thing I hadn't thought to do, and thus another unwelcome sign that I'd lost a step.

I was really too old for this shit.

I brushed the thought aside. I hadn't seen anybody enter or leave the building, and as far as I could tell I was the only lurker on the block. I went across the street and buzzed the super.

When he answered, I gave my name. He said he'd be right up.

"No, just buzz me in," I said. "I'll come down to your place."

At least I remembered the route. I found the back staircase, walked down to the basement. Henry Loudon met me at the foot of the stairs and led me back to his apartment. He'd just made coffee, he told me, and would I like a cup?

I let him pour me a cup, and when I complimented him on his coffee he launched into a riff about how he was fussy about coffee, and where he bought the beans, and the brewing method he'd settled on. Then he stopped abruptly and apologized for going on and on.

"You want to know about Miss Lipscomb,"

he said. "I don't think she's been back. Though she could get in and out and I wouldn't necessarily know about it."

Actually, I said, I was more interested in the man.

"The one who's not her brother. Haven't seen anything of him, either. I'd have told you if I did."

"And no phone calls?"

He shook his head.

"That's just as well," I said. "He won't be expecting a call from you."

"You want me to call that man?"

I explained what I had in mind, and he was clearly troubled. I asked him what was wrong.

"I don't even have his number," he said. "Gave you that slip of paper."

"I have the number, Henry."

"That's the least of it, anyway. My mama raised us not to tell lies."

"Well, in special circumstances—"

"Oh, it's not the right or wrong of it. It's the training. Comes to lying, I'm just not very good at it. I get flustered, and what I say comes out sounding untruthful."

"A little practice," I said, "will make all the difference."

WE MUST HAVE SPENT fifteen minutes rehearsing. I sketched out a script for him, and we took turns playing Henry and Paul. By improvising, he learned to come up with responses to anything Paul was likely to say, and as he settled into the role he grew a lot less flustered.

We finished our coffee, and he put the phone in his breast pocket and checked to make sure he had the right key, and I got my backpack onto my shoulder, then took it off again and asked him if he had a spare roll of duct tape.

He said, "In this job? That's like asking a pharmacist does he have any aspirin."

He never asked me what I was going to use it for, just gave me a roll, and threw in a scissors without my asking. I added both to my backpack. We went upstairs, walked down the hall to the front staircase, and climbed three flights of stairs. When we'd both caught our breath, he opened the door to Ellen Lipscomb's apartment. There was a light switch alongside the door, but I left it alone. We had all the light we needed.

I took him one more time through the conversation he was going to have, and he took a deep breath and made the call, then rolled his eyes when it went immediately to voice mail. But we'd rehearsed this, too, and he said, "This here's the super on East 27th Street. Call me back real quick."

He pressed what you press to end a call, took another deep breath, and right about then his phone rang. He looked at me and I nodded.

He answered the phone, said, "Super."

We could have put his phone on Speaker, but that might have made it harder for him to play his role. So I only heard one side of the conversation.

"She's here," he said. "Your sister. Just a few minutes ago. Rang my bell, said she lost her keys, needed for me to let her in. Uh-huh. Uh-huh. Well, I don't know exactly how I could stall her, so might be best for you to get here as soon as you can."

He listened, said *Uh-huh* a few more times, then rang off and asked me how he'd done.

"From what I heard," I said, "you could get an Emmy nomination."

He grinned at that. "He didn't seem suspicious at all. Said he'd get over right away. I said just buzz me and I'll be right up."

"So you'd better get downstairs."

"What I was thinking. No, you don't need to do that."

What I didn't need to do was hand him a pair of hundreds, and he was probably right, I probably didn't need to do it. But maybe it would help keep him from forgetting which side he was on.

"Said he's got keys, picked up a spare set of hers. I never saw him do it."

"You just saw him take the panties."

"God, don't remind me. I'll keep an eye on the door, call when he's on his way. If I can."

AFTER HE'D LEFT, I opened the backpack and took out the two items I'd purchased. One was a black silk ski mask, the kind that fits over your whole head, with two small almond-shaped holes for your eyes and a larger one for your mouth. The other was a kitchen mallet with a ten-inch hardwood handle and a head of hard black rubber, one side of the head capped with a toothed disc of cast aluminum for tenderizing meat.

Waiting was the hard part. I wanted to put a light on, move around the apartment. Instead I donned the ski mask, to check the fit, and promptly took it off again; it was all too good at warming one's face. I hefted the mallet, swung it gently into my palm, first with the plain rubber end, then with the toothed metal. That was my dress rehearsal, I thought, and waited for it to be showtime.

I didn't have long to wait. Fifteen, twenty minutes,

and my phone vibrated in my breast pocket. I picked up, and in a hoarse whisper Henry told me our man was on his way. "Didn't see me," he said. "Doesn't know I saw him."

He rang off before I could say anything.

I listened for footsteps. I didn't hear him on the stairs, but picked up his footsteps as he approached the door. I stationed myself so I'd be behind the door when he opened it.

He took his time getting the key in the lock. Then he turned it, and then he eased the door open and stepped into the apartment.

He was a big man, taller and heavier than I, dressed in ironed khakis and a navy blazer. I don't know what he sensed, her absence or my presence, but the set of his shoulders shifted, and his hands moved at his sides. So he was on guard, and I might only get one crack at him.

I took it, swung the mallet into the back of his head.

For longer than I expected, he stood there as if rooted. I'd pulled the punch the least bit, not wanting to shatter his skull, and maybe that had been a mistake. Then, when I drew back the mallet for another try, his knees buckled and he hit the floor and didn't move.

"EVERETT ALLEN PAULSEN. He was carrying a New Jersey driver's license, and it had his name in full. The rest of his ID, mostly credit cards, was all either Allen Paulsen or E. Allen Paulsen."

Elaine said, "And he called himself Paul. I wonder what he has against the name Everett?"

"Or Ev for short," Ellen said. "Or, I don't know. Rhett?"

By the time I'd got home Elaine was ready to leave for the Croatian church. Could I make myself a sandwich? Was I okay with that? I was fine with it, I assured her, and when was it her meeting ended? Nine o'clock? Well, could she come right home afterward? And could she bring Ellen?

I never did fix myself that sandwich. I spent a long time under the shower, most of it with the hot spray hitting me in the back of the neck. I got dressed and sat down in front of the TV, and I guess I must have dozed off. But if I was sleeping it couldn't have been very deeply, because my eyes snapped open when I heard Elaine's key in the lock.

And now the three of us were in the living room, but this time it was I who shared the couch with Elaine, while Ellen Lipscomb perched on my recliner. I took them through my day, and I may have furnished more detail than they needed to hear about my fruitless quest for a nightstick and the kitchen mallet I'd rung in as a substitute.

I'd have been more concise a few years earlier. An old man's like an old river, tending to meander, given to lingering in the interesting bends and curves it cuts into the earth. A couple of times I had to remind myself to move the narrative along, that my trip to the Bowery didn't require a whole disquisition on the history of that venerable thoroughfare, including the spelling of its original Dutch name.

Still, neither of them looked bored.

"So I swung at him," I said, "and if I hadn't pulled it a little at the last moment I think I'd have killed him."

"But you didn't."

"I knocked him cold," I said, "but it took a couple of long seconds for his body to get the message. He stayed upright and looked to be bracing himself, getting his feet under him, and if he'd managed to turn around—"

"He'd have seen a man in a ski mask," Elaine said.

"And he'd try to take the mask off, and my head along with it. He was big, and he had to be strong to take that initial blow. And I'm an old man."

"Not that old," Ellen said.

"Old enough to feel a lot better when his knees buckled and he hit the floor. Old enough that I had to catch my breath before I taped his wrists behind his back and rolled him over."

And went through his pockets, and found his wallet, and learned his name.

"Everett Allen Paulsen," Elaine said, testing the name on her tongue. "It's like Rumpelstiltskin," she told Ellen. "Now that you know his name you'll never have to worry about him again."

Ellen wanted to know if that was true. Could she stop worrying about him now that she knew his name?

"I think so," I said, "and knowing his name's only a part of it. Not just his name, but knowing his home address in Teaneck. His office is on 56th Street just east of Broadway, I've got both addresses written down. And he knows I know who he is, and where to find him."

"After you went through his wallet—"

"I waited for him to come to. He wasn't out that long, just a few minutes. Then his breathing changed but his eyes stayed shut. I waited him out and eventually he butched up and opened his eyes."

"And beheld the Masked Avenger," Elaine said.

"It should have been reassuring."

"Why? Oh, because if you were going to kill him you didn't have to keep him from seeing your face."

I nodded. "But the sight must have scared him."

"It would have to. He must have thought he'd found his way into a comic book."

Ellen asked what happened next.

"I talked to him. I told him he could never come to your apartment again, or call you, or make any attempt to get in touch with you. I told him if he ever did any of that, I'd find him and I'd kill him."

"And he believed you?"

"Maybe not right away. The first thing he did was protest his innocence. He didn't know you, he never threatened you, and he swore to God and everybody he wouldn't do it again."

" 'I never borrowed from you a pot,' " Elaine said, in an unconvincing Jewish accent. Ellen looked puzzled. I knew the reference, but decided it could wait.

I said, "I didn't want to listen to it. I put a couple of strips of duct tape over his mouth. That scared him, because it meant we weren't going to have a conversation. I think he knew what was coming."

"An unfortunate accident," Elaine said, answering Ellen's unspoken question. "Your Mr. Paulsen fell down a flight of stairs."

"You threw him down the stairs? What if somebody saw you?"

"It's an expression," I explained. "Years ago there would be times when a cop took something personally. Hauling the perpetrator down to the station just wasn't enough. So you'd take it out on him with your fists or your boots, and the explanation for his injuries would be that he fell down a flight of stairs.

"And sometimes," I remembered, "it was the literal truth. Vince Mahaffey and I caught a domestic in Park Slope, neighbors called it in because of the screams coming from the apartment. Hulking brute of a husband, little mouse of a wife, and he's done a good job of beating the crap out of her."

Elaine was nodding, remembering. I'd told her the story, possibly more than once.

" 'Oh, it's nothing, officers. I'm clumsy, I fell down, I tripped over something, it happens all the time, it's all my fault.' In other words, no, she won't press charges. We talked to the neighbor who'd made the call, and weren't surprised to learn this happened a lot. She almost didn't call, she said, because there'd been cops there before, and the same thing always happened. The husband denied everything and the wife insisted it was an accident and he never laid a finger on her. So she usually just let it go and tried to tune it out, but this time it was worse than usual and she was afraid he'd actually kill her.

"I said I guessed there was nothing we could do.

Mahaffey said, 'Fuck that shit,' and went back to the wifebeater's apartment and hauled him out of there. 'She won't press charges,' he said. 'You're wasting your time.' Mahaffey said maybe she wouldn't press charges, but he was charging the son of a bitch with resisting arrest. 'What resisting? What arrest?' And Mahaffey took him to the head of the stairs and tossed him. He missed more steps than he hit, but he hit plenty and he landed hard, and he was pissing and moaning and yelling that something was broken, and Vince got him to his feet and threw him down another flight. The apartment was on the fourth floor, I remember that, because the bastard went down three flights in all."

"Your partner threw him down three flights of stairs?"

"Two," I said.

"But you said—"

"You can blame the third flight on the Masked Avenger," Elaine said. "Am I remembering it right? He wanted you to have a hand in it, didn't he?"

"So I couldn't report him for it," I said, "but I never would have done that, and I'm sure he knew it. I think it was more that he wanted us to share the act. And he didn't want me to miss out on something he thought I'd enjoy."

"And did you? Enjoy it?"

"*Enjoy* might not be the right word," I said. "But I have to say it was satisfying. Mahaffey picked him up afterward and cuffed him, and the poor bastard was sure there was more coming, but he just hauled him out of there and we put him in the back seat of the squad car. 'You want to go around resisting arrest,' Mahaffey told him, 'you ought to hold off until you're a little better at it.'"

BUT I HADN'T PITCHED Paulsen down a flight of stairs, although the image was not without appeal.

What I did was give him a beating. I used my feet more than my hands, and I left his face alone. I did things that wouldn't show unless he took his clothes off. I kicked him in the ribs and the groin and the kidneys.

"I had to force myself to do it," I remembered. "What a lot of people will do is work themselves up, build up a load of hate. The guy they're working over is the worst man in the world, and they're doing God's work by kicking the shit out of him. I couldn't manage this. He wasn't an evildoer who had to be punished. He was a problem that had to be solved."

Elaine: "And this would solve it?"

"If he was completely delusional, like the woman

who dropped in on David Letterman, then probably not. Or if he was a stone psychopath who didn't think in terms of consequences. But he wasn't quite that crazy. He was fixated on a particular woman in a dangerous way, an unacceptable way." I looked at Ellen. "He wasn't going to stop stalking you, and sooner or later he'd find you."

"But you found him first."

"And I needed to hurt him, and scare him, and make it clear to him that you weren't worth the trouble. At one point I paused to kneel down next to him and told him how he was going to behave from now on. 'You can never call her again,' I said. 'You can never go near her apartment. You can never look for her, or hire someone to find her. You can never write her a letter. If you see her on the street, you'd better turn around and walk in the opposite direction.'"

"Or otherwise you'd hunt him down and kill him."

"Yes."

"And he believed you?

I'd crouched over him, my forearm across his throat. I'd leaned just a little of my weight on him. *I could kill you right now*, I'd told him, and increased the pressure a little.

"Yes," I said. "He believed me."

—ww—

AFTER A BEAT SHE said, "And would you? If he turns up again, if he stalks me, what would you really do?"

"What I said I would."

"You'd kill him?"

Killing hasn't been a big part of my life, and I've never taken it lightly. I can only think of one instance when it occurred after I'd been able to take time to think about it. The man was named James Leo Motley, and in a sense he brought Elaine back into my life, and for that I might have been grateful to him.

But he did so by flying out to Ohio to rape and murder her friend Connie Cooperman, and then he came back to New York and killed a bunch of other people. He capped it by stabbing Elaine, and very nearly killing her. The crew in the Emergency Room saved her, but it was touch and go for a while.

I wound up in the apartment where Motley had touched down, and he wound up unconscious after I'd almost wound up dead. I hated him, not surprisingly, for what he'd done and what he tried to do. But I didn't kill him out of hate, or out of a desire to see him punished.

But I knew that, even if he went back to prison, there would be a day when he got out. And he'd go on doing what he'd been doing, because that was what he did and who he was. There was really only one way

I knew to stop him, one way that was sure to work. If there was another, I couldn't think of it.

And so I did what I had to do.

"I don't think he'll give you any more trouble," I told Ellen. "But if he does, yes. I'll find him and I'll kill him."

ELLEN HAD TO USE the bathroom, and Elaine went off to the kitchen and started water boiling for pasta. They'd come straight home from the meeting, she said, and hadn't eaten. I admitted that I hadn't either.

"Plus you had an arduous day," she said, "with all that walking, and then kicking the crap out of whatshisname."

"Everett Allen Paulsen," Ellen supplied. "I guess his last name is where the Paul came from."

"Probably."

"You're right about Rumpelstiltskin," she said. "It's empowering, knowing his name. You didn't leave him there, did you? In my apartment?"

"No. I took off the ski mask, because I'd stopped caring if he saw my face. Then I took the tape off his mouth and got him up on his feet. He couldn't really walk, he could barely stand up, but I put an arm around his waist and walked him down the stairs."

Elaine said that must have been tricky.

"The Mahaffey method would have been a lot easier," I said. "I had trouble keeping my balance, so a couple of times we both came close to taking a tumble. And it was a little dicey when we ran into somebody on the stairs. I said my friend had a little too much to drink."

"And he believed it?"

"She," I said. "Five-seven or eight, slender build, late twenties. Dark hair, eyeglasses—"

Ellen thought she knew who I meant, but not her name. "She usually has her earbuds in," she said, "so she probably didn't hear a word you said."

"I got him downstairs," I went on, "and I walked him to the corner and put him in a taxi. I told the driver a similar story, that my friend wasn't feeling too well. His main concern was that the son of a bitch would puke in his cab, but I assured him that wouldn't be a problem, my friend wasn't drunk, he had this condition from injuries sustained in the service of his country. He'd have spells like this periodically, and the only thing that helped was quiet and rest."

"So don't ask him questions," Elaine said.

"I gave the driver Paulsen's address in Teaneck and a hundred bucks to cover his fare. And off they went."

"And you came home."

"Not right away. First I went down to the basement to let Henry know everything was settled, and he wouldn't be seeing any more of your brother."

"Her faux brother," Elaine said. "Didn't Henry see you schlepping Paulsen down the stairs?"

"I think he made a point of staying in his apartment. He was relieved to have it all over with, and happy to lend me the key rather than go upstairs with me."

"You went back upstairs?"

"To straighten up, and to retrieve what I'd brought with me. Oh, that reminds me."

I went to the other room and returned with the backpack. I had dropped a like-new kitchen mallet in one trashcan and a worn-once ski mask in another, so there was only one item in the backpack, and I took it out and handed it to her.

"My alligator bag," she said.

"I didn't know what else you might need or want," I said, "and when I started looking around, it felt like an invasion of privacy."

"You might have found panties," Elaine said. "Can I see? Oh, it's a beauty. You wouldn't want to leave this behind."

"I thought I would never want to look at it again,"

she said, and clutched the handbag to her chest. "Because he touched it."

"Oh, for Christ's sake," Elaine said. "He had his hands all over your pussy, too, and you're not gonna get rid of that, are you? This is a gorgeous bag. You hang on to it."

THE PASTA WAS THE sort that looks like little bedsprings. Fusilli, I think it's called. It was topped with Paul Newman's marinara, which Elaine had pepped up a little with Dave's Insanity hot sauce. She'd thrown together a salad, too.

"My default setting," she said. "Pasta and a salad. It's a good thing everybody likes it, because it's the only thing I ever seem to cook."

No one complained. Hunger's the best sauce, even better than Paul's and Dave's, and we all brought good appetites to the table.

Afterward we had our tea in the living room. Ellen talked about her apartment, and tried to figure out if she wanted to return to it. "Just in case he's crazier than we think," she said, "maybe I shouldn't be too easy to find."

"On the other hand," Elaine pointed out, "it's rent-stabilized, isn't it?"

"For the next eight months. Then the built-in increase takes it over the edge, and the landlord can ask full market value for it."

'Then the hell with it," Elaine said. "You can live anywhere."

"I can, can't I? I like where I am now, on the Upper West Side. I'll stay there for the full period of the sublet, and by then I might be able to find something in the neighborhood. Or Brooklyn, which seems to be where everybody is moving these days."

"Except for the ones moving to Harlem, or the South Bronx."

"I really could go anywhere, couldn't I? Figuring out where I want to live is the least of it. What I really have to figure out is who I want to be."

"No rush on that one," Elaine said.

"No. That woman this evening, the one who's going back to school? I could do that."

"I wouldn't make her a role model just yet." They both laughed, and to me Elaine said, "She told us how she blew her professor to get her grade changed."

"But it wasn't really prostitution," Ellen said, "because she didn't take any money for it."

"And besides she really deserved an A."

"Plus he was sweet, and she might have done him anyway."

....

—*mm*—

"SPEAKING OF MONEY," Ellen said, "you spent a lot of it. I want to pay you back."

I told her not to worry about it.

"But that's not right," she said. "A hundred dollars to the cab driver, and I don't know how many hundreds you gave my super. Plus the mallet and the mask and the backpack, and why should you be out of pocket for all that?"

"I'm not out of pocket," I told her. "Quite the reverse. I came out ahead."

"How do you figure that?"

"Our friend had more in his wallet than ID and credit cards. He had over eighteen hundred dollars, most of it in hundreds and fifties."

"And you took it."

"Just the large bills."

"Good for you," Elaine said. "What do we need with chump change?"

SHE REFILLED OUR TEACUPS, and then the two of them got to talking about other things various Tarts had said. In AA this would have been considered breaking a person's anonymity, but Tarts didn't have

....

AA's formal traditions, and anyway I didn't know the people they were talking about.

"I don't know why men want to see two women together," Ellen said. "Would you get off on watching two guys?"

Elaine said she wouldn't, but she'd read that a fair number of straight women enjoyed watching gay male porn. But she couldn't believe it was anywhere near the proportion of men who were turned on by lesbians.

"No, I'm sure it's not." To me she said, "Is it a turn-on for you? Two women?"

"It doesn't make me want to run out of the room," I said.

"A lot of clients wanted it," Elaine said. "What they wanted was a date with me and a friend of mine, but they always wanted us to fool around a little before they joined in."

"Did you like dates like that?"

"They were okay," she said. "I never felt romantic about a girl, but I didn't mind the sex part."

"That's what I was thinking of, when it's romantic. What that one woman said."

The woman in question, I learned, was a lesbian. Her girlfriend was also in the game, so when a client wanted a threesome that was who she recruited, and they put on a show and did each other, and then they both did the guy.

"Like you do," Ellen said.

"And it ruined her relationship," Elaine said. "Once they'd turned their lovemaking into a performance, it wasn't fulfilling anymore. It made them self-conscious, as if someone was watching them."

"With his dick in his hand," Ellen said. "They broke up not long after that. And the ironic thing is that the main reason she picked her girlfriend for the date was because she thought it would be cheating if she brought in another girl."

I'd wished I could be a fly on the wall at a Tarts meeting, and this was even better.

Elaine told how her regular partner on threesie dates had been her best friend in the game. "And if anything we were closer friends afterward."

"Because you'd shared the experience."

"Not just that. She was cute and funny and very sweet, and I'd had thoughts about her. Not fantasized exactly, but, you know, wondering what it would be like."

"To be in bed with her."

"Uh-huh. And it was nice. Matt probably knows who it was."

I said I could probably guess. "Connie Cooperman?"

"Yes, and all of a sudden I'm so sad I could cry."
To Ellen she said, "She met a real nice guy and got married and moved out to—was it Indiana?"

"Ohio," I said.

"And then someone went out there and murdered her and her whole family. I don't want to think about it."

ELLEN SAID, "YOU SAID something earlier. In a Jewish accent."

Elaine didn't remember, but I did. "The woman who borrowed the pot," I said.

"Oh, right. So there are these two dames, and one accuses the other of borrowing a pot from her and never returning it. And the second woman denies everything. "In the first place, I never borrowed from you a pot. In the second place, it was an old pot. And in the third place, I gave it back to you in better condition than you gave it to me. It's not really much of a joke. It's better as a reference than a joke."

"The way you used it."

"Right."

One thing it did, it got the spotlight off Connie Cooperman.

ELLEN ASKED IF A client of Elaine's ever wanted to bring her home to his wife. Never, Elaine said. She'd heard enough stories along those lines, but nobody ever invited her to that sort of party.

Ellen said, "Really? I would get that a lot. And, you know, it was a different experience every time. Once it was obviously all his idea, and his wife hadn't had any experience with women and didn't particularly want to. She was just helping him fulfill his fantasy."

"Accommodating of her."

"Another time the wife had a lot more experience with girls than I did, and knew just what she wanted to do. And another time . . ."

The energy in the room had changed. All this sexually-charged talk, I thought. It could hardly fail to raise everybody's temperature.

But it was more than that.

Ellen shifted in her chair, crossed her legs. She said, "There was this one couple."

"Oh?"

"He was a nice guy. A lot older than me, like really a lot. And I'd had two or three dates with him, and he said he knew his wife would like me, and how would it be if the three of us went out for dinner?"

Elaine: "Like a date? I mean a date date?"

"Kind of. Still, it was pretty clear how the date

was supposed to end. I put on a good dress and met them at a really nice restaurant. I mean, not some ridiculous place with a $200 tasting menu, but a decent French restaurant. I couldn't tell you what I ordered, but I remember it was good, and so was the wine."

She paused, thinking back, and not about the food or the wine.

She said, "I don't know why, but I expected his wife to be closer to my age than his. I was wrong about that, she couldn't have been more than a few years younger than him. But she was still pretty, and she'd kept her figure."

"An attractive woman of a certain age."

"And very sweet, and completely at ease. The food was excellent, and the conversation was about everything in the world but what we were there for. He was a Yankees fan and she was a Mets fan, and they said they were living proof that a mixed marriage could work out. There was a Tom Stoppard play on Broadway, and they'd seen it and so had I, and we talked about that. We never ran out of things to talk about. It was a great conversation and a terrific meal, and afterward we sipped our espresso, and nobody wanted an after-dinner drink.

"And she said, 'Ellen, we like you very much. Would you like to come back to our apartment?'"

"I guess you went."

"You think? Their apartment was just a block or two from the restaurant, and it was a beautiful night, and we walked there. Not too fast and not too slow, because we really wanted to get there but the anticipation was too exciting to hurry through it. Do you know what I mean?"

I knew what she meant.

"It was like electricity in the air, that kind of energy. They lived in a full-service building, of course, with a doorman *and* an elevator operator. They were on the twelfth floor, and he unlocked the door and locked it again when we were inside, and she took me in her arms and told me how sweet and pretty I was. Then she kissed me, and I got all caught up in the kiss, and then she let me go and he took her place, kissed me on the mouth and then on the side of my throat, right at the pulse point. He had his arms around me, and then she was touching me, too.

"I never said their names, did I?"

"No."

"Gordon and Barbara. Their apartment was gorgeous. Antique furniture from different periods. Art on the walls. He pointed out a couple of paintings, told me things about the artists, but I couldn't take it in.

"There was soft indirect lighting in the bedroom.

The bed was queen-size, and it had been turned down. He took off his jacket and hung it over a chair, and she turned so that I could help her with the zipper of her dress. And when we'd all taken off all our clothes, she looked me up and down, and her face just filled up with delight, and I honest to God felt like the most beautiful woman in the world.

"She came over to me, and put a hand on me. No one had said a word since we entered the bedroom, but now she spoke. 'Let's do everything,' she said."

"IT WAS KIND OF magical," she said. "Very highly charged sexually, but there was something else going on, too, something primal. I felt as though I was healing something from my childhood, some trauma I didn't even know was there. I remember there was one moment, I was lying on my back and they were on either side of me, not touching but close enough that I could feel the warmth of their bodies. And I felt safe. It was like I'd never in my life felt completely safe, and now I did."

Elaine asked her if she'd stayed the whole night.

"Most of it. I didn't fall asleep, nobody slept, and there was a point where it felt like it was time to leave, and nobody tried to talk me out of it. I got dressed and Gordon handed me an envelope and offered to take me downstairs and put me in a cab, but he'd have had to get dressed and I knew the doorman could get me a cab.

"I went home and went to bed, and I must have fallen asleep within minutes. And when I woke up I felt this strange combination of happy and sad, and it took me a while to realize that the sad part was because I knew I would never see them again."

"But you did," Elaine said.

"How did you know? What happened was they sent flowers, not that day but the day after. Just their names on the card, Gordon and Barbara. No message."

"The flowers were the message," Elaine said.

"Yes, but I wasn't sure what it meant. 'We had a wonderful time and we never want to see you again.' I wanted to pick up the phone and thank them for the flowers, but I didn't know what was appropriate, or what they might want. There'd been a thousand dollars in the envelope. A thousand dollars plus a good dinner, plus flowers."

I said, "Well, you paid for your own cab."

"Plus I tipped the doorman, and the kid who brought the flowers, if we're keeping score. Anyway, I didn't make that phone call. And a couple of days later, when I'd stopped wondering if I'd hear from them and accepted that I wouldn't, the phone rang and it was Gordon.

"I told him the flowers were lovely, and how sweet it was to send them. And he said something about the importance of finding a really good florist, which was certainly a subject I'd never thought about, and then he asked if I'd be able to see them Saturday evening.

"I didn't need to think. I said I'd love it, but there was one condition. I didn't want to take any money for it. He said not to be silly, and I said I wasn't being silly, and I made it clear that I was serious. And we arranged a time for me to come over.

"And I got there a few minutes early, so I made myself look in a store window for a while and then go to their building. He answered the door wearing a sport jacket but no tie, and she was in lounging pajamas, which was a very good look for her. Kisses right away, and then a little petting on the living room couch, and then we got up and headed for the bedroom. And just before we crossed the threshold I said, "I have one request, but if it's too weird just say so and we'll forget I ever said it. But would it be all right if I called you Mommy and Daddy?""

THEY WERE FINE WITH it, she told us. It added something, not that anything needed to be added, and not that she could define what the extra element was. She saw them three more times at intervals of about a month, and after the last time she left knowing they wouldn't be calling her again.

She looked off into the middle distance, at a memory or a notion. Then she looked at each of us in turn, and said, "It's true, in case you're wondering. Everything I said is exactly what happened."

I started to say something, but she held up a hand and stopped me.

"Exactly what happened and how it happened," she said. "But here's what you should know. I'd have told you that story even if I'd had to make up every word of it."

Nobody dropped a pin. I would have heard it.

"I've never seen your bedroom," she said. "Is your bed big enough for three?" She smiled. "Oh, come on," she said. "You know you want to do it."

WHEN I OPENED MY eyes, it was because the morning sun was streaming through the window. It generally does that, except on overcast days, but I rarely notice because I always sleep on the far side of the bed. So it was disorienting, and it took me a moment to realize that our normal sleep routine had been altered, and how and why.

I turned, and saw Elaine on the other side of the bed, sleeping on her side, facing away from me. I was relieved and disappointed, in approximately equal parts, that it was just the two of us. I closed my eyes, turned away from the daylight, and would have gone back to sleep if my bladder had let me. I got up and went to the bathroom, and when I got back in bed Elaine was awake.

I said, "Did that happen?"

"Either that or we both had the same vivid dream. You know how it's always a mixed blessing to live out a fantasy in real life? I mean you're glad you did, and it's exciting, but it's never quite as good as it was when all you were doing was imagining it."

"Not necessarily."

"That's where I was going," she said. "Just a few days ago we imagined the whole thing, and we had a good time—"

"More than a good time."

"—and what we just did was better. I don't want to talk it to death, but it's got to be right up there on my list of peak experiences."

"Probably not all that far from the top."

"Not far, no. Did you see it coming? Because I didn't."

"Once she started telling the story about the older couple—"

"The much older couple."

"Oh, ever so much older.

"Gordon and Barbara. Gordie and Barb?"

"Gordo and Babs," I suggested. "By the time they were in the restaurant, I had a feeling where she was going."

"Oh, sure. By then."

"But even then," I said, "I wasn't close to certain."

"Because we'd fantasized about it."

"So I figured we were like one of those predatory pedophiles who's convinced the child is flirting with him."

"That's a flattering analogy." She rolled her eyes. "And I'm not about to feel guilty, even if we are twice her age. That child had a serial orgasm that lasted almost as long as the war in Vietnam."

I said, "While we're on the subject, where is she?"

"Probably home, and I hope that means the uptown sublet and not 27th Street. She climbed over me to get out of bed, and I kind of woke up, and I'm pretty sure I heard the shower running."

" 'I'm gonna wash that couple right out of my

hair.' She probably went home. Unless she's napping on the couch."

"Or sitting in the recliner with her feet up, reading the *Bhagavad Gita*. I don't see her clothes."

"Can't you read the *Gita* with clothes on?"

"Yoga pants, maybe. We're being silly." She got out of bed, and a few minutes later I heard the shower. She returned wrapped in a towel and holding a sheet of paper.

"On the coffee table," she said. " 'That was wonderful. I love you both. Call me sometime.' "

"Do we have to send flowers?"

"You'd have to call Gordon, because he knows it's important to get a really good florist. No, I don't think we should send flowers." She looked at the sheet of paper. "Not 'Call me,' " she said. " 'Call me sometime.' Which is to say we can but we're not obliged."

"What do you want to do?"

"I want to make coffee and fix breakfast," she said. "Oh, about Ellen? It doesn't hurt a bit that I really like her."

"So do I."

"And I'm not exactly her sponsor, and anyway this isn't AA, so I don't see any reason why I can't fuck her."

"As a matter of fact, you may be helping her stay away from prostitution."

"One day at a time," she said. "So what I think we should do is exactly what she said. Call her sometime."

"I like your thinking. And if she wants to call us Mommy and Daddy?"

She cocked her head. " 'Mommy and Daddy.' Jesus. Still, who knows? We might even like it."

It's Getting Dark in Here
By Lawrence Block

AGES AGO, LUCILLE BALL had this exchange on *I Love Lucy* with a snobbish character whose task it was to elevate her culturally:

SNOB: "Now there are two words I never want to hear you say. One is *Swell* and the other is *Lousy*."

LUCY: "Okay. Let's start with the lousy one."

Funny what lingers in the mind…

―――

EVERY YEAR OR SO, I stub my toe on a couple of buzzwords and decide I'd just as soon not encounter them again. There are two that I've found increasingly annoying of late, and if Lucy were here I'd tell her that one of them is *Awesome* and the other is *Iconic*.

It is in the nature of the spoken language for words to come and go, and none are more cyclical than those we choose to indicate strong approval or disapproval. *'Swonderful*, Cole Porter told us, that you should care for me. Indeed, *'Smarvelous*, isn't it? *Wonderful, marvelous, terrific, sensational, excellent, brilliant*—each takes its turn as a way of demonstrating great positive enthusiasm.

For quite a few years now, *le mot du jour* has been *awesome*. Now it's a perfectly reasonable word, and means simply that the noun thus modified is likely to inspire awe, even as that which is *wonderful* is clearly full of wonder. If everything thus described is truly awesome, one is left to contemplate a generation of wide-eyed and slack-jawed folk gaping at all that is arrayed in front of them.

Well, okay. Periodically a word of approval swims upstream into the Zeitgeist, resonates with enough of us to have an impact, and becomes the default term for us all—or at least those of us under forty. Before too long its original meaning has been entirely subsumed, and all it means to call something *awesome* is that one likes it.

Deep down where it lives, *awesome* is essentially identical in meaning to *awful*. And there was a time when *awful* and *wonderful* were synonyms—full of awe, full of wonder. Now, as Lucy could tell you, one is swell and the other is lousy.

If anything good is *awesome*, then anything memorable or distinctive is *iconic*. I shouldn't complain, I don't suppose, as several of my own books have had that label applied to them, and perhaps I ought to regard the whole business as awesome. But iconic? Really? No narcissist thinks more highly of his own work than I, but I have trouble picturing any of my books as a literal icon, displayed on the wall of a Russian Orthodox cathedral.

Wait, let me rethink that. Maybe *Eight Million Ways to Die* might make the cut. I mean, dude, that book is *awesome*.

NEVER MIND. I HAVE the honor to present to you seventeen stories, any or all of which you might well describe as awesome or iconic or both. And I want to introduce them by pointing out another buzzword, one of which I've tired at least as much as I have of the two of them combined.

Noir.

It's a perfectly good word, and particularly useful if you're in Paris and an ominous feline crosses your path. "*Un chat noir!*" you might say—or you might offer a Gallic shrug and pretend you hadn't seen it. Whatever works.

Noir is the French word for black. But when it makes its way across *la mer*, it manages to gain something in translation.

Early on, it became attached to a certain type of motion picture. A French critic named Nino Frank coined the term *Film Noir* in 1946, but it took a couple of decades for the phrase to get any traction. I could tell you what does and doesn't constitute classic film noir, and natter on about its visual style with roots in German Expressionist cinematography, but you can check out Wikipedia as well as I can. (That, after all, is what I did, and how I happen to know about Nino Frank.)

Or you can read a recent novel of mine, *The Girl With the Deep Blue Eyes*. The protagonist, an ex-NYPD cop turned Florida private eye, is addicted to the cinematic genre. When he's not acting out a role in his own real-life Film Noir, he's on the couch with his feet up, watching how Hollywood used to do it.

That's what the French word for black is doing in the English language. It's modifying the word *film*, and describes a specific example thereof.

Now though, it's all over the place.

The credit—or the blame, as you prefer—goes to Johnny Temple of Akashic Books. In 2004 Akashic published *Brooklyn Noir*, Tim McLoughlin's anthology of original crime stories set in that borough. They did very well with it, well enough to prompt McLoughlin to compile and Akashic to publish a sequel, *Brooklyn Noir 2: The Classics*, consisting of reprints. It did well, too, and a lot of publishers would have let it go at that, but Akashic went on to launch a whole cottage industry of darkness.

A look at the publisher's website shows a total of 120 published and forthcoming Noir titles, but the number is sure to be higher by the time you read this. Akashic clearly subscribes to the notion that every city has a dark side, and deserves a chance to tell its own stories.

It is, I must say, a wholly estimable enterprise. I could not begin to estimate the number of writers whose first appearance in print has come in an Akashic anthology. They owe Akashic a debt of gratitude, as does a whole world of readers.

And as do I. I had the pleasure of editing *Manhattan Noir* and *Manhattan Noir 2*, and while neither brought me wealth beyond the dreams of avarice, each was a source of personal and artistic satisfaction. And, after I'd coaxed a couple friends into writing stories for my anthology, I could hardly demur when they turned the tables on me. I'd written one myself for *Manhattan Noir*, and wrote another for S.J. Rozan's *Bronx Noir*, and a third for Sarah Cortez and Bootsie Martinez's *Indian Country Noir*. All three were about the same cheerfully homicidal young woman, and although she didn't yet have a name, she clearly had a purpose in life. I found more stories to write about her, realized they were chapters of a novel in progress, and in time *Getting Off* was published by Hard Case Crime.

So I wish their series continued success. Although their stories have never had much to do with Hollywood's 1940's vision of *noir*, neither are they happy little tales full of kitty cats and bunny rabbits. They are serious stories, taking in the main a hard line on reality, and any gray scale would show them on the dark end of the spectrum.

Noir? Noirish? Okay, fine. I'm happy for them to go on using the word. In fact I'm all for letting them trademark it, just so the rest of the world could quit using it.

That, Gentle Reader, is a rant. And you can relax now. I'm done with it.

．．．

—*mm*—

SO HERE WE HAVE seventeen stories, and you'll note that they cover a lot of ground in terms of genre. Most are crime fiction to a greater or lesser degree, but James Reasoner's is a period Western and Joe Hill's is horror and Joe R. Langdale's is set in a dystopian future, and what they all have in common, besides their unquestionable excellence, is where they stand on that gray scale.

They are, in a word, *dark*.

And that, I must confess, is the modifier I greatly prefer to *noir*.

It's easy to see I'm partial to it. A few years ago I put together a collection of New York stories for Three Rooms Press, and the title I fastened upon was *Dark City Lights*. (While I was at it I fastened as well upon some of that book's contributors; of the writers in *At Home in the Dark*, six of them—Ed Park, Jim Fusilli, Thomas Pluck, Jill D. Block, Elaine Kagan and Warren Moore—wrote stories for *Dark City Lights*.)

The title came to me early on. Years ago I'd come across O. Henry's last words, spoken on his deathbed, and in case you missed them in the epigraph, you needn't flip pages. "Turn up the lights," said the

．．．

master of the surprise ending. "I don't want to go home in the dark."

I CAN BUT HOPE you enjoy *At Home in the Dark*. I find it's inspired me, and there's another anthology taking shape in my mind even now. I already have a title in mind, and it's five words long (as my titles tend to be), and it has the word *dark* in it.

Trust me. It'll be awesome.

• • • • •

At Home in the Dark
(*Available Spring 2019*)

My Newsletter: I get out an email newsletter at unpredictable intervals, but rarely more often than every other week. I'll be happy to add you to the distribution list. A blank email to lawbloc@gmail.com with "newsletter" in the subject line will get you on the list, and a click of the "Unsubscribe" link will get you off it, should you ultimately decide you're happier without it.

Lawrence Block has been writing award-winning mystery and suspense fiction for half a century. His newest book, a sequel to his greatly successful Hopper anthology *In Sunlight or in Shadow*, is *Alive in Shape and Color*, a 17-story anthology with each story illustrated by a great painting; authors include Lee Child, Joyce Carol Oates, Michael Connelly, Joe Lansdale, Jeffery Deaver and David Morrell. His most recent novel, pitched by his Hollywood agent as "James M. Cain on Viagra," is *The Girl with the Deep Blue Eyes*. Other recent works of fiction include *The Burglar Who Counted The Spoons*, featuring Bernie Rhodenbarr; *Keller's Fedora*, featuring philatelist and assassin Keller; and *A Drop Of The Hard Stuff*, featuring Matthew Scudder, brilliantly embodied by Liam Neeson in the 2014 film, *A Walk Among The Tombstones*. Several of his other books have also been filmed, although not terribly well. He's well known for his books for writers, including the classic *Telling Lies For Fun & Profit* and *Write For Your Life*, and has recently published a collection of his writings about the mystery genre and its practitioners, *The Crime Of Our Lives*. In addition to prose works, he has written episodic television (*Tilt!*) and the Wong Kar-wai film, *My Blueberry Nights*. He is a modest and humble fellow, although you would never guess as much from this biographical note.

Email: lawbloc@gmail.com
Twitter: @LawrenceBlock
Blog: LB's Blog
Facebook: lawrence.block
Website: lawrenceblock.com

CPSIA information can be obtained
at www.ICGtesting.com
Printed in the USA
LVHW042111211119
638113LV00006B/1171/P

9 781795 663021